I0618883

Sex and Insensibility

HEARTS OF LOUISIANA, BOOK ONE

MAGGIE PRESTON

CYPRESS PRESS, LLC

Title: SEX AND INSENSIBILITY / Maggie Preston
Description: Paperback First Edition
Publication Date: September 21, 2023
Cover Design: Fantasia Frog Designs
Formatting: Samantha Moran, Obsidian Inkwell Publishing, LLC

Paperback ISBN-13: 978-1-7356234-3-6
Also available as an ebook edition.

All art and logo copyright © 2020 by Maggie Preston

About the Purchase of This Book

Contents

To Deb, for making me believe I could do this.

Chapter One

Technically, Lara Caldwell Haley's ex-husband died *before* she hit him with the Buick.

At least that's what the coroner had said.

"I guess now you won't have to go through with the divorce," her mother announced, unwinding the crime scene tape that circled the porch. Helen Caldwell believed in a positive attitude.

Lara leaned against the stair railing for support. "Mom, the divorce would be final on Friday. Brian and I were just waiting on the paperwork." Lara had also been waiting on Brian to finally move out.

"I know. Still..." Helen let the sentence hang, but Lara could finish it in her sleep. *What will people think?*

According to Lara's mother, Caldwells didn't get divorced. Caldwells married well. Caldwells were fruitful and multiplied. Caldwells lived happily ever after. It was the Caldwell way.

Lara decided long ago she must be adopted.

It was moments like now, as her next-door neighbor samba-ed her way between the uneven boxwood hedge separating the two properties and beneath the crime scene tape flapping like a NASCAR caution flag around the driveway, that Lara truly struggled with her commitment to the Caldwell way. Did Lara run into the house and pull the shades to hide? Nooooooo. Her mother should be proud.

Gently, Lara reached over and rubbed a leaf of her uprooted camellia plant now lying on the porch rather than in the garden where it belonged.

"What really gets me is that he tried to steal my camellia."

It, too, was wrapped in crime scene tape, though the police had decided against taking it in as evidence. Unlike the Buick, which they kept impounded. They'd also asked if she had any plans to leave town, which left her a little discombobulated. She'd been in Belle Terre her entire life. Was she allowed to leave?

Her mom shook her head thoughtfully as if in answer to the question but said instead, "It was a beautiful camellia."

The next-door neighbor gave a semi-heartfelt *tsk-tsk-tsk* to show her sympathy as she waddled up the walkway.

"Such a pity."

Lara ignored the woman, hoping she'd go away. Another *tsk-tsk-tsk* let her know it didn't work.

"Such a pity."

"So *young*." Candy dragged out the last word. "So very young. Then again," the neighbor through the tight grimace of a disapproving scowl, tapping one bloodred nail against her chin, "you were divorcing him, so maybe you don't care."

Lara swallowed the not-so-ladylike retort hovering near the tip of her tongue. It would be un-neighborly. Helen Caldwell's daughter would never say such things. She might think them, but...

Lara sighed and looked to the October sky for strength

or divine intervention. Neither seemed likely at the moment. She took the higher road, as she'd been taught since childhood. "Of course I care, Candy. Just because the divorce was almost final doesn't mean I don't care."

Even with the three-year separation and pending divorce, he'd been her husband. She wanted to feel something more for the man she'd married, but she didn't. It wasn't something she was proud of but it was the truth.

"Guess Brian should have gone to see my Douglas like he was supposed to. Yep. He should have seen Douglas. If he'd just gotten that checkup, he might not be"—the neighbor paused, cupped her hands around her mouth then whispered loudly—"*dead*."

She whispered it as if Lara didn't know Brian was dead. Or the hundred other people that had stood vigil on the curb yesterday morning to watch her life fall apart didn't know he was dead. Or the police or the medical examiner or her family didn't know he was dead. It was just that some words were unspeakable in public unless whispered. *That* was the Southern way. The Caldwells didn't have influence over everything, no matter what her mother may think.

"You're right, Candy." What else could she say? Brian was the poster child workaholic. Of course, thinking back to the text messages she had recently discovered on an old cell phone, Lara had reason to question how much of that time he actually spent *working*.

Candy and Helen seemed to wait for Lara to say or do something. For the life of her, Lara couldn't figure out what. She always did what was expected of her. She'd dated the boys her friends expected her to date. She'd married the man her parents expected her to marry. She'd tried to be the wife her husband expected her to be.

Whose expectations was she supposed to live up to now?

Maybe it was time to stop trying. The idea appealed to her. Angelina Williams, the award-winning best-selling romance novelist filling the front window of the downtown bookstore where Lara worked, wouldn't care about other people's expectations. Her heroines were break-the-rules women. Lara hadn't broken many rules in her life. At least not that anyone knew about.

Candy bent over and plucked a wilted petal from one of the camellia blossoms, yanking Lara back from the edge of deep thought on rebellion. Lara cradled the bush protectively against her breast, curling her fingers around the branches. She'd been fighting for this plant for three years, the sole point of contention in her divorce.

Brian had given her the house, something she didn't think was right because it had belonged to his parents, but in exchange he'd wanted her Debutante antique camellia. The court finally ruled in her favor on ownership of the plant so, taking matters into his own hands, he'd tried to steal it during the night when four generations of heart disease and a back seat of fast food wrappers caught up to him.

Rubbing the petal between her fingers, Candy nodded thoughtfully. "Camellias are just too delicate. Too delicate. That's why I like the hibiscus."

Helen nodded her silent agreement as she stuffed the yellow tape deep into the trash can, arranging a paper bag carefully over the top before securing the lid. She straightened, swiping her hands together triumphantly. "They're the way to go with our soil and weather."

Lara agreed as well, but she'd planted the camellia a few years back and entered the Carnival Flower Show. She'd been winning first prize ever since.

She inhaled the heady fragrance and dragged a finger

along the ridge of a soft pink blossom. A thing almost too delicate to touch came from such a sturdy branch, the leaves a protective shield, the roots deep and strong.

"But the roots are still good." Lara said it out loud to herself more than anyone and the sound of her voice cleared her head. Her own blossom may be a little wilted at the moment, but she had good roots, even if they were a bit tangled and exposed.

She looked to Candy and her mom, feeling more sure of herself than she had since the nightmare began yesterday morning. "I think I can replant and still save the bush." Lara refused to let anyone see her down. She'd kept her head up for the last three years. She could hold it up for another three minutes or until she got inside her house, whichever came first. She was a Caldwell, after all.

Candy bobbed her head like an apple at the Halloween carnival scheduled for tomorrow night. "Perhaps, perhaps. Plenty of water might do the trick. Yes, it might do the trick, but I wouldn't count on it." The bobbing morphed into a spring-loaded shake. "No. I wouldn't count on it."

Her mom studied the plant carefully and the fake smile spread across her face. "You should try, dear. Caldwells never give up."

Her mother had said the same thing when Lara told her about Brian's cheating and asked if she should save her marriage. "You think I can save it?"

That fake smile again but her mom was silent this time. Maybe Helen knew when to walk away as well.

"Well then." Lara pushed to her feet, the camellia still cradled in her arms. "Looks like I'll have to sit out the flower show this year."

Apparently the news appealed to Candy, who had a wall full of second-place ribbons. "I'm sure that's the best decision for everyone." Not to let the moment of victory go too soon, she crinkled her face into a self-satisfied smirk. "I also hear Mr. Lautner is going to sell his book store to that big construction company." Candy held her hands out for emphasis. "Big construction company."

LCB Development. The name soured in the back of Lara's throat.

"Didn't you want to buy it some years ago? Can't say I'm sorry. Nope. Can't say that. Of course, I can't believe you work there, either. Some of the books he sells in that store. Really, Lara. What does your mother think?" Candy looked to Helen for support, but Helen was focused on the crime scene tape around the driveway.

"I'm sure Mr. Lautner wouldn't allow anything *inappropriate* in the store," Helen countered somewhat sheepishly, obviously caught between family loyalty and community support.

Candy gasped, fluttering a hand in front of her face as if the mere thought of an *inappropriate* book set her soul aflame.

"Nothing but pornography if you ask me." Candy vibrated with more of the spring-loaded shake. "Por-nog-ra-phy."

The self-satisfied smirk stabbed Lara right in the gut, but Candy's defamation of The Book Nook brought a heated flush to her face. She pushed to her feet. "It's not por-nog-raphy." She put a little waggle to her hips to accentuate each syllable then continued with more dignity at her mother's wide-eyed but silent reprimand. "It's romance." She left out the adjective "erotic." No sense feeding fuel to Candy's self-righteous fire.

The book store was in one set of seven stores along the riverfront. The land and building were jointly owned by a co-op of owners, all of whom had to agree with the sale to LCB Construction. As it was now, there was one owner withholding their vote to sell. Lara hoped that was enough for the moment to keep LCB from moving forward with their proposed AmeriMart store.

"Hah! Those Angelina Williams books you love to put in the front window are pure smut. Smut! I would never read such a book."

Lara cocked one hip and settled her hand on her waist. "How would you know they're pure smut, Candy, if you've never read one?"

Candy sucked back the words about to leave her mouth, momentarily stunned by the little flaw in her logic. She looked to Helen for moral support but didn't find what she was looking for, so she continued. "I don't have to put my hand on the stove to know it's hot."

Lara wasn't going to say anything to that. Her mother wouldn't approve of the snarky comments going through her head. The old Lara would have let it go. Given the spiraling disaster of her life, however, maybe it was time for a new Lara.

"I've never really like you, Candy. How about we just avoid each other from now on?"

Oops. Was that my out-loud voice? Yes, it was, and she wasn't sorry. Candy had come looking for gossip. Now she had it.

"Lara!" Helen exclaimed in her best motherly tone.

Candy's face exploded in a crimson that would have looked lovely if her lips weren't pursed to blueness. "Well I never!"

"I know," Lara said mostly to herself. "I never do that. All these years I kept those things to myself. Feels kinda good to let them out."

Candy's eyes narrowed into an expression that clearly stated, *I'm going to tell everyone you said that,* then she whirled her pudgy self around and torpedoed back through the crime scene tape and uneven boxwood border.

And Lara knew she would. Not much happened in Belle Terre that people didn't know about from one source or another.

"That wasn't very kind, Lara," her mother chastised, her gaze following the retreating form of the neighbor back through the uneven hedge. "And when are you going to do something about that hedge?"

Lara sighed before she could help it. When all else failed, ignore the truth. Even Lara had managed that tried and true tactic because the hedge was a horticultural disgrace. One half was a good four inches taller than the other, with rounded sides where the shorter sides were perfectly squared, a seven-foot-long monument to testosterone and the Solomon-like legal system that seemed to work in her hometown.

"Brian and Douglas couldn't agree on whose property the thing sits."

"Oh, well then, okay. Guess I'll go home for now, but I'll be back later to check on you."

Helen gave her a quick peck on the cheek and made her way back down the street to her own home just a few blocks away.

What now? Lara wondered. She'd been in some type of relationship her entire life. Daughter. Girlfriend. Wife. Her résumé was fairly limited, but it was what her family expected. Now she was just Lara.

The relief she'd expected to come when her marriage finally ended didn't settle around her. Lara just felt alone, but that was pretty much how she'd felt during the last part of the marriage, too, so she figured she would cope. Maybe there were Oreos in the house. That usually helped her coping skills, especially since she didn't drink. Maybe she could start drinking as well. Just a bit.

Lara shook her head and sighed again before she could stop it. She fanned her face, trying to stir up some semblance of air to cool the burn on her cheeks. A store like AmeriMart would destroy the family businesses in Belle Terre, and as much as Lara questioned her life at the moment, she loved this town. It was the last semblance of normalcy left to her. Someone had to do something.

Maybe it was time for a change. Did the Caldwell way allow for change? She doubted it, but she hadn't done a lot of the things the Caldwell way lately. Maybe she was on a roll and just didn't know it yet.

Chapter Two

As Lara's gaze lifted from the uneven shrubbery separating her house from Candy's, she noticed the medium-sized moving van parked in the drive of the Hastings' place. The Hastings hadn't lived there for almost two years now. It took time to get used to change in Belle Terre.

"Frick." She blew away the curl of hair falling over her left eye. "New neighbors."

Lara swept her gaze down Chestnut Lane, a street normally filled with kids on bikes and skateboards but one that today stood empty. At least her part of it.

There was no way out of what must happen next, Lara decided. It was her duty, her obligation. She'd been raised on those two words, and Helen Caldwell's daughter would never let anyone down. Helen Caldwell's daughter *had* never let anyone down—except that one time, her mind countered. Besides, it gave her something to do other than feel sorry for herself.

Lara turned toward the house that she'd lived in for the last ten years. The perfectly symmetrical line of pansies on each side of the gaping hole where her camellia used to live.

A plaque with the family name emblazoned in crisp white letters over the door. So perfect. It all rang untrue to her now, she realized sadly.

Lara thought she'd loved Brian; thought they would have a life like she'd envisioned. A life like her parents and brother and sister. A normal life. She'd worked hard to build that kind of life for the two of them. It was what Caldwells did.

Brian had been the one to rope her into the Belle Terre Ladies Auxiliary for Family Values. It was only after she'd agreed to be on the Welcome Wagon committee that she discovered Brian didn't do it out of a sense of community or a commitment to family values. He'd done it to get invited to the mayor's monthly appreciation luncheons. Almost all of Brian's investment accounts were born at one of those luncheons. He'd used her to make business contacts. Since the mayor was also her brother, Lara wondered if the marriage had been about business contacts as well, but she'd agreed to be on the committee, and Caldwells never went back on their word.

Then again, she'd been a Haley for ten years. Was there a statute of limitations on family commitments?

Lara didn't think so.

So Lara carefully set aside the broken camellia and went to make a pitcher of lemonade. Anytime a new neighbor moved in, someone brought a pitcher of lemonade and a plate of homemade cookies to the family. It was Lara's turn. The entire committee knew it was Lara's turn so they expected...Lara was beginning to dislike that word. But with so much else out of control in her life right now, it was something she could focus on.

Once inside, Lara opened the cabinet with more zeal then she would have thought possible at the moment and pulled the door off at the hinge. Her breath rushed out in a huff with only a hint of anger. Lara closed her eyes, rested her head against the cabinet, and counted silently to ten.

When she could face it again, Lara opened her eyes and looked around her mother-in-law's kitchen. It had always been her mother-in-law's kitchen. Brian wouldn't let her change a thing. Broken tiles hidden by dishtowels, the cracks in the linoleum that could no longer masquerade as part of the pattern, and the wallpaper twenty years past outdated. Brian had never been the fixer-up type. Why had she waited for him to do it all these years?

Because he was supposed to do that kind of stuff. She was supposed to do the cooking-cleaning-babymaking stuff. That was the southern way.

"Two out of three ain't bad." But even Lara could hear the regret rumble from her heart and settle around her words. She'd never been able to get pregnant, as Brian often reminded her.

The ache jolted sharply and she widened her eyes to keep the layer of tears from spilling over her lashes. The pain twisted a little deeper, though, as she realized that her chance for a family dwindled now even further. Did they let single women suspected in their husband's death adopt children?

Glancing out the kitchen window, she turned over the ruin of her life in her mind—the broken marriage, the broken promises, the broken camellia, the uneven hedge separating her property from the neighbor.

Another unladylike sigh.

She dragged her thoughts from the hedge to the lawn that stretched between the house and the street, still green in the warm autumn air that swirled up from the Gulf. The carpet of St. Augustine was manicured to perfection and

Lara thought of the kitchen falling apart on the inside. The outside was what mattered in her world.

It was time to make some changes in her world, she decided. Time to take charge of her own destiny.

The phone rang, interrupting her destiny change. Lara stared at it, hoping whoever held onto the other end would go away.

Rrriinnggggg.

Lara answered the phone somewhat reluctantly. "Hello?"

"Lara?" the familiar voice asked cautiously. "It's Sally."

As though, after fifteen years of marriage to Lara's brother, Paul, she wouldn't recognize her sister-in-law's voice. "Hi, Sally."

"How are you doing, honey?"

Well...my camellia bush is kindling. I have PMS. We have new neighbors and it's my turn to make the lemonade. Oh...and yesterday I ran over my almost-ex-husband with the car. But I'm taking charge over here.

"I'm okay."

Liar, liar, pants on fire.

Lara stashed the broken cabinet door behind the refrigerator. *Never underestimate the power of denial in an emergency.* She cradled the phone between her ear and shoulder and retrieved her Welcome Wagon pitcher and platter from the top shelf of the cabinet.

"Vera Chambers called. She heard from Candy's mother-in-law's sister's nephew who works for the sheriff's aunt that you were under arrest down at the police station."

"Not exactly, Sal." Lara opened the refrigerator and stared at the contents. "The police just have a lot of questions in a case like this. I was going to call, but I needed to make some lemonade first." She found the bag of lemons in the drawer of the refrigerator and removed the sugar canister from its perch over the stove. A broken tile gaped at her from the now-empty spot. Lara moved the flour canister in front of it.

"Lemonade?" The intonation in Sally's voice didn't raise a decibel. Nothing ruffled Sally Caldwell unless she wanted to be ruffled. Being married to the mayor of the small town, she'd had to develop a killer poker face. "Maybe I should come over."

Almost the entire neighborhood and most of her family had arrived yesterday before the police and asked twice as many questions. The police could take a lesson or two from the Caldwells about the third degree.

"Everything is under control." *Said the lookout to the captain of the Titanic.* "Give my love to Paul."

Lara hung up the phone before Sally could protest and stared at the pitcher, lemons, and sugar sitting on her countertop. She liked pink lemonade, but no one liked pink lemonade around Belle Terre. It was like pink flamingos on your lawn or white sandals after Labor Day. It simply *wasn't* done.

She opened the refrigerator and stared again. A gallon of orange juice. Half a head of lettuce. Unopened pack of bologna. The usual condiments, including five bottles of assorted mustards. Brian liked mustard and bologna. The combination made her cringe, but she'd done her wifely duty, at least in that regard, and kept the fridge stocked with mustard and bologna. She looked at the grocery list on the freezer door.

Wednesday was always grocery day, but she'd been little preoccupied yesterday and the Piggly Wiggly in Donnelly didn't stay open late during the week. Mondays were laundry. Sundays and Fridays were housework. Thursdays were gardening. Afternoons and Saturdays she spent at the bookstore.

The bookstore.

Still staring at the lack of contents in her fridge, Lara let out another sigh, but no anger this time. Only regret.

Lara had never met the faces behind LCB Construction, nor did she ever want to. She'd read enough to know they were the fastest growing land development company in the country, and starting next week, they would be in Belle Terre. That is, if the building permit got approved by the city council.

The city council meeting was tomorrow night right before the fall carnival opened. Never let it be said the town leaders weren't practical in their scheduling. Maybe she should go down there. Just to see what was said. It was her civic duty, and Lara knew everything there was to know about duty.

She might not be able to save the bookstore, but she could take charge of the Welcome Wagon duties. She retrieved the lonely gallon of orange juice and dumped it into her Welcome Wagon pitcher. Tiny bubbles escaped the surface. No lightening. No hand of an Almighty Being swooping down to *thwap* her on the head.

Hmmmmm.

It was a small rebellion in the life of a dutiful daughter and former prom queen, but even the small rebellions tingled like a revolution.

From the broken cabinet, Lara retrieved a new bag of double-stuffed Oreos—her personal favorite, which made her sacrifice even greater—and emptied the bag onto the platter. She scooted them around a little so they had the look of thoughtful arrangement.

Lara stepped back to eye her creation. Store-bought

orange juice and Oreo cookies. The Ladies Auxiliary would probably have her drawn and quartered. At the very least, they'd take away her official Welcome Wagon pitcher and platter.

Let them try, Lara silently vowed, protectively gathering her orange juice and Oreo cookies and stalking toward the door. *I have PMS and a Buick. Any questions?*

Crossing the front yard, Lara glared at the uneven boxwood hedge. "You're next."

That rebellion sparked a little easier. Maybe it was time for Helen Caldwell's daughter to find a few more rebellions. But where to start?

The newfound defiance put a confident lilt in Lara's step and she glided across Chestnut Lane toward the new neighbors. She would play nice for a few more minutes. Then, watch out, Belle Terre.

The back of the moving van was open, revealing not so much as one stick of furniture. Instead, a monster Harley Davidson motorcycle sat secured to the interior of the vehicle.

Stainless steel trim. Aluminum frame. Speedo face. Sixteen-inch wheels. Knucklehead engine.

"Now that's a hog." She whispered the words with the reverential awe such a thing inspired.

A slice of her past flashed through her brain. The rumble of the bike between her legs. The sinewy strength of the body pressed to her chest. Roving hands. Gentle lips.

What good was a rebellion if you didn't kiss a few rebels?

The memory swirled around her for a moment. Now *there* was a rebel she should have been bad with. Lara needed to be bad. Really bad. Downright naughty, even. Angelina Williams would know what to do. Too bad her rebel was no longer around and Angelina Williams only lived in the bookstore.

She knocked on the door, lost in the memory of something that never was, wondering what it would be like to give in to those fantasies. Lara thought of the rows of romance novels lining the shelves of The Book Nook. The women in those books would have gone for it. They would have loved the guy on the motorbike, no matter what their parents said.

Life is not a romance novel, Lara. Fantasies don't come true in Belle Terre.

The door lock turned and Lara tried to remember to smile graciously over her store bought orange juice and Oreo cookies. It was the thought that counted. Right?

All thoughts left her as the door opened and she found herself face-to-face with the rebel himself.

"Frick."

Chapter Three

Will Kenner couldn't remember if he'd actually been asleep when the annoying pounding began. He didn't think so. It was the only way he could explain the vision standing on the front porch, holding Oreo cookies and...orange juice?

He scrubbed at his eyes, feeling every one of the thousand miles he'd driven yesterday scratch behind the lids. The two hours of sleep didn't do much to clarify the vision, either. He hoped he'd remember to pull on some pants before answering the door.

It must be exhaustion, he reasoned. Hints of perfume, something outdoorsy and sexy as hell, crowded out the reason and Will slid his hand back to swipe the hair from his line of sight. The vision cleared, but did not float away on the cloud of curls circling her head. Familiar sea-green eyes narrowed and Will watched the moment of realization click in her brain.

The platter of Oreo cookies teetered on her fingertips, and before the surprised O fully formed on the mouth that haunted his memories, Will reached out and steadied the platter in her hands. "It would be a sin to waste all those Oreos." A few other sins were coming to mind, however.

Will let his gaze drop, remembering a certain cheerleading uniform, a certain pair of legs hiked around his waist as they roared out of town on his '44 Vincent Black Knight, a certain kiss he'd briefly tasted and still imagined now and again.

Slim ankles were tucked neatly into the pristine white sneakers, but most of her legs were hidden by shorts that fell just above her knee. What a shame. From what he could tell, she still had killer legs.

"Will?" The rush of his name between her perfect lips stirred things left unstirred for years and pulled his gaze back up to her mouth.

He leaned against the doorframe, slipping one hand inside the front pocket of his jeans, thankful he'd remembered the pants. He let the smile widen on his face. "Are you my official welcome to Belle Terre?"

The vision swallowed and Will watched the muscles in her slim neck work. She opened her mouth to speak, and Will was again riveted to the movement of those lips.

"Maybe you don't remember me. I'm—"

Will stepped into the vee of her arms, the cold pitcher pressing against his bare stomach, and reached out to her. He let his hands hover at the sides of her face, not touching, but close enough to feel the flush of her skin. Her pupils widened in the lush green of her eyes. Dark lashes fanned out above and below, near-perfect half-moons only a shade or two darker than the crown of curls. Then Will did what he'd wanted to do since he'd kissed her when he was seventeen years old.

He kissed her again.

He let his lips whisper over hers for a moment, tasting

her, drinking in the sweetness of her soft mouth against his and drowning in the memories. She tasted of home and acceptance, things he'd never known as a kid. Things he'd been looking for as an adult.

Will leaned closer, touching her face with only the tips of his fingers. He felt her gasp. Saw her eyelids flutter closed. Felt her lips part slightly. Her face warmed. Her lips moved. Her body trembled against his. She smelled of fall—cool, crisp. He trailed his hands down the slope of her neck and shoulders, then the upper arms.

The rapid intake of her breath, each shuddering release trembled against his skin. He finally settled his hands on her waist, his fingers spreading to encompass the slender roundness of her hips, the slight swell of her buttocks. His body turned to liquid fire and she melted into him, and for the first time, Will wanted to be seventeen again, to start over and take a chance. He sucked in a breath to cool the desire, but it only fueled the fire.

He broke the kiss but let his eyes linger intimately on her face. Her eyes fluttered open and something glistened in the green—passion, confusion. He couldn't tell which. If it was possible, she was more beautiful today than she was fifteen years ago. "Lara Caldwell."

Her eyes widened. How could he forget the girl that stole his heart? But she didn't know that.

"Let me take those." Will plucked the orange juice and platter of Oreos from her hands and ducked back into the house. More than his mind was concentrating on Lara. His body entertained a few wicked thoughts of its own, tightening in places where the heat seemed to coil around his insides.

What the hell was he thinking?

He'd come back to Belle Terre with one purpose—to

prove he had changed. So what did he do to start out on the right foot? He'd molested the first woman he'd come in contact with. Oh, but it had been worth it.

The swell of her cotton T-shirt brushing against his bare chest. Tan, firm legs that went a mile past eternity. The spattering of freckles she no longer tried to hide with makeup. She was the most beautiful thing he'd seen since the last time he laid eyes on her.

The door closed behind him and Will wondered which side of it she was on. A warmth hovered over his skin, the memory of her nearness, close enough to feel but not close enough to burn.

"It's Haley now."

Ouch. He should have known she'd be married by now. There were plenty of men out there her parents would have approved of for their daughter. He had never been one of them. Not Royal Kenner's boy.

But that was a long time ago. Right?

And she didn't seem opposed to his kiss. Of course, he'd kind of taken her by surprise. Looking into her eyes moments ago, time stood still. She was still eighteen, high school prom queen, cheerleader, newspaper editor, his best friend's sister, off-limits. He was still seventeen, resident bad boy, outsider, juvenile delinquent, off-limits.

Will set the pitcher and platter down on the only available flat surface in the living room, a box labeled "essentials." He slipped into a button-down shirt lying nearby but didn't button it, his body angled toward her, while she stood statue-still and avoided his gaze. Lara looked lost standing there in the empty shell of his house. He didn't remember her ever looking so un-Lara-like. Not even fifteen years ago when he kissed her that night by the lake.

"By the way," he said to fill the silence, "congratulations."

"Congratulations?"

"On your marriage."

"Oh." She pushed at a wayward curl. Will wanted to twirl it around his fingers and pull her close for another kiss. "Oh! That! I am...or was...but I'm not anymore...I don't think."

It was Will's turn to be confused. "I think I need a drink. How about you?"

"I don't really drink." Lara's shoulders dropped and the words rushed out on the tail end of a sigh. A weak smile touched lips still moist from his kiss.

That mouth again. Will needed to stop thinking about her mouth, especially if she was married, but then again, she didn't sound so sure about the marriage thing, so maybe he could think on it a little longer.

Will shifted the cookie platter to the floor and opened one side of the "essentials" box. He withdrew two glasses, and half-full bottles of vodka, sloe gin, and Southern Comfort. Some things you should never be without.

After he'd retrieved some ice from the kitchen, he nodded his head at the cooler situated by the boxes. "It's as close to furniture as I have right now. Have a seat."

Without a word, Lara folded her body down onto the cooler, crossing her legs at the ankles and tucking her feet to the side.

He opened the bottles and poured them into the pitcher of orange juice, eyeballing the measurements. Will served up a liberal portion and handed it to Lara, then poured himself one. When he turned back around, Lara had her glass up-ended, draining the last of the drink. She handed him the empty one and took his.

"Thanks." Her eyes said, *I needed that.*

"Don't mention it." His body said, *No, keep talking.* "You said something about being married?"

Sadness floated on a wave of tears that would not crash over her lids, but it dissipated almost as quickly as Will noticed it.

"We separated about three years ago." Lara took a sip.

"I'm sorry."

"But he wouldn't move out at first, and it was his parents' house." She paused to sip her drink. "And I didn't really have anywhere to go except home, and that would have never worked out." More sipping. "You remember my mother."

He nodded, letting her talk. She seemed to be getting the hang of the drinking thing, too.

"And...well...he sort of died." Lara took a longer sip this time.

Will's jaw dropped. "Died?"

"Yesterday." This one was worth two sips, apparently.

"Yesterday?" He was starting to sound like a myna bird, so he closed his mouth and let her talk.

"The coroner wasn't really sure about the time, but he was certain Brian died before I hit him with the Buick."

Lara held out her empty glass toward him. Will filled it, adding to his own glass as well. He leaned against the entryway column, close enough to touch but sensing she needed some space so the story could pour out. He mentally divided the information he now had.

Lara Caldwell is still in Belle Terre. That's good.

Lara Caldwell is now Lara Haley. That's bad.

She's been separated for three years. That's good.

She apparently hit her dead husband with a Buick.

Will wasn't sure which side of the line to put that little

piece of information, so he just filed that under the heading, "Reasons not to let Lara drive."

Will didn't like the look in Lara's eyes—fear, danger, trapped. The tremble in her limbs reminded him of a doe caught in the crosshairs. Will wanted to erase the look from Lara's face and didn't want to see that fear cross her features ever again, and he *never* wanted to be the one to put that look there.

"Another drink?"

"Oh yes, please." She gestured to the moving van visible through an opening in the drapes. "I see you still like your bikes." *I still remember that night.*

"Some passions never die." *That was the best and worst night of my life.*

"I'm surprised you remember me." *I've never forgotten you.*

"Why are you surprised?" *I've never forgotten you, either.*

"I don't know." She looked un-Lara-like again, uncertainty creasing her face and tensing along the subtle lines hugging her mouth. "I just never expect anyone to remember me."

"I remember you." He heard the drop in his voice and a familiar tightness coiled in his chest. Something had stolen Lara's spirit over the years. Something. Or someone. Will put his money on the *someone*. "I'm sure everyone remembers you."

Lara looked away as the uncertainty swallowed her. "I haven't had a drink in a really long time." She took another long sip and again Will watched the muscles in her neck, letting his face follow the arch of her throat to the open vee of her T-shirt. She licked her lips then added, "Brian said it was unladylike."

Brian. The *someone* in question, no doubt. Will hated

him instantly. Not for marrying Lara, not for being good enough in the eyes of her parents to marry Lara, but for not treasuring her once he had her. The rest he could forgive, but the latter...Of course, Brian was dead. It was hard to hold a grudge against a dead man. Will had tried for years.

Lara interrupted his thoughts. "Does this drink have a name?"

The rapid change in the tone of her voice left him a little dazed, as if something rushed by quick enough to steal the breath from his lungs. Tension prickled along his skin.

"I love drinks with names, not that I drink, but today... today I feel like having a drink with a name."

Will smiled, slowly letting the grin broaden on his face. "It has a name."

She took another long sip, watching him over the rim of the glass. Waiting.

Finally, she prodded him. "Well?"

Patience never was a virtue with Lara, but then again, in high school she'd never had to wait for anything she truly wanted. Will wondered if anything had changed. He moved closer to her. "It's called a Sloe Comfortable Screw."

Lara's mouth formed that cute little *O* again and a rosy flush brightened beneath the spattering of freckles. He stopped with less than an inch between them, the air suddenly energized and warm as if the two of them this close together created heat and other forces of nature. Will leaned down and took the glass from Lara's hand, not afraid she would drop it but afraid she would crush it in the white-knuckled press of her fingers.

Will couldn't resist and went in for the kill. "Are you ready for another?"

Chapter Four

Spontaneous combustion seemed possible at any moment. How could Will look so...so...darn *calm* while he stood there and propositioned her?

Calm wasn't the right word, though, as Lara tried not to watch the way his skin rippled and moved, sliding over muscles that said "hard work" rather than "health club." And he hadn't moved an inch. He just stood there, watching her watch him. Oh, there was the smile that teased one corner of his mouth and brought out the lopsided dimple in his cheek, a smile that sing-songed wickedly, *I know what you're thinking.*

Of course, maybe he wasn't propositioning her, and a certain amount of disappointment washed over Lara.

He pressed a refilled glass into her hand, then tucked his left hand in the front pocket of his jeans, letting the other fall to his waist where the movement shifted the ice in his glass. His upper body had faint tan lines around the arms and neck, like he only wore his shirt part of the time, and Lara couldn't drag her thoughts back from visions of him without his shirt.

"A penny for your thoughts." That easy, relaxed voice pulled Lara from her wandering thoughts.

"You'd better bring your Visa card." Her mouth went dry, but Lara resisted the urge to lick her lips. That might look like an invitation.

She licked them anyway.

Lara wanted Will to proposition her. Like that night at the lake. With her cheerleading sweater pushed high over her ribs, her hands tangled in the leather of his bad-boy jacket, his thumbs brushing the white cotton of her bra. She always wore white cotton back then. Ladies wore white cotton and didn't guzzle drinks with names like a Sloe Comfortable Screw.

But then again...times they were a-changing.

"No credit cards." Will looked at her beneath the fall of sleep-tousled blond hair too short to be fashionably long and too long to be intentional.

"You could write me a check. Of course, I'd have to ask for some identification." She tried for humor but failed miserably. His gaze made her aware of every inch of exposed skin, and given the sensible nature of her outfit, there wasn't much. Still...wherever he looked, heat followed.

"You know who I am, Lara." His voice deepened, thick with unspoken words, and something she didn't want to name reflected behind the chocolate depths of his eyes. Will was light and dark, water and oil, fire and ice. He was everything you wanted but nothing you expected. She'd fought that knowledge in high school, caught between the expectations of her family and friends and what she knew to be the truth behind Will Kenner. Lara didn't want to fight it anymore.

"I know, Will."

Her voice sounded breathy, shallow, maybe because her

heart leapt up to lodge in her throat. Or maybe it was sliding lower. Her body pulsed, hummed with a rhythm all its own. Parts that hadn't hummed in years were now playing The Flight of the Bumblebee. Words and emotions tied themselves around her brain and Lara struggled to put them into something intelligent. She pushed to her feet, suddenly needing to be vertical, but the world swayed and Will reached out to steady it.

"Did you just wake up?" So much for intelligent, but she was out of her element, an unusual but not unwelcome state of being for a person who'd always done the expected.

"Yes." The darkness in his eyes lightened with the quick smile that told her he was willing to let the conversation turn away from its course. At least for now. "I drove in last night and made it here just before dawn."

"What brings you back to Belle Terre? Business or pleasure?"

"The first, mostly." He lifted the glass to his lips, then paused. "But I'm not opposed to some of the other."

His response touched off a firestorm in the pit of her belly. Things tightened. Nerves tingled to life. Lara shook away the wandering thoughts like the remnants of a bad dream. But it wasn't a bad dream. It was real. He was real.

As if moved by her thoughts, Will shifted his weight from one leg to the other. The motion caused hair the color of summer wheat to fall over his forehead and brush the arch of his eyebrows. The gold in his hair, deeper now than it had been years ago, caught what sun filtered in through the overhead skylights. Something slid behind his eyes and darkened the brown to polished mahogany. Lara shivered as the old memories brushed over her skin.

I think this is the part of the movie where we ride out of town on your bike.

As long as it's also the part of the movie where I finally get to kiss the girl.

The rush of night air through the silk of his hair had carried the scents of soap and summer rain and beneath that something stronger pulling her close to his body. He smelled like home. Not her home, not the house she shared with her parents, but something that could have been all her own. All their own.

The confusion must have been a tangible force in her eyes, because Will put down his drink and narrowed the distance between them. He didn't walk. He glided, as if he had muscles where he shouldn't and his bones were made of something fluid but strong.

Lara swallowed and took another sip of the drink but didn't taste it. She should leave, she told herself, at least hold out her hand to stop his predatory approach, but she didn't. Lara wanted to be the object of his attention. She wanted everything his eyes promised, if only this once. Scarlett O'Hara had one thing right—she'd think about the consequences tomorrow.

Will continued to glide toward her, slowly, as if the distance between them was some great chasm and not just a few feet of carpet. Like he wanted to reserve his energy for things other than walking.

"Is this new carpet?" she asked, breathless.

Lara let her gaze move up his body, following the line of sinew and muscle visible beneath Will's open shirt. A light matting of hair widened from where it appeared at the waist of his jeans. Shadow and light played on the flat plane of his abs and the edge of his ribs. Then there was his chest...

"I think it's new carpet."

Why couldn't she take her eyes away from his chest?

Because you haven't had sex in three years.

That had to be it. She'd seen him bare-chested in high school, but with stolen glances and secret looks. Lara didn't want to be secretive anymore, and with Will, she knew she could be the person lurking beneath the surface. Maybe life was giving her a second chance to be the person she was supposed to be.

"Berber carpet." Why was she still prattling on about carpet? Because she wanted to talk about his body, and the look he was giving her. She'd not been looked at like that since the last time Will looked at her that way. It still brought forbidden thoughts to her mind.

The glass grew cold to the touch, or maybe her hands were growing warmer. As that thought fluttered through her brain, Lara followed the warmth in her hands as it traveled up her arms, across her shoulders to crash like a tidal wave into her face and down her torso. Heat mingled in her belly, coiled around her insides and tightened until she had to open her mouth to draw breath.

Lara noticed for the first time that his jeans weren't buttoned and rode low on his hips, held up not by luck but by other, more pressing matters.

The distance faded until only a deep breath of space separated them. Lara could not raise her eyes to meet his, afraid of what she would see. More afraid of what *he* would see.

She'd let him down when they were kids. They weren't kids anymore, but Lara was still afraid of letting him down. She wasn't the same person she had been all those years ago. She didn't know who she was, but she wanted to find out.

Will raised his hand toward her and Lara froze inwardly, afraid of the touch but wanting it nonetheless. Will lifted his hand and placed the tip of his finger beneath her chin, tilting her head back until she could do nothing but look into his eyes.

"About that night...Will, I'm sorry. I should have—"

Will put his fingers to her mouth. "It was a long time ago." He ran the pad of his thumb over the bottom curve of her lip. "You still have the most beautiful lips. I should have stolen more kisses when we were kids."

Breathing became optional and Lara heard herself say, "There's nothing stopping you now." It was brazen and wanton and so unlike her, and she liked that it wasn't like her.

It was the invitation he needed because Will leaned in and whispered against her lips. "I guess there isn't."

The kiss hovered over her mouth, only a thought, a desire flaring between them like heat lightning in the summer sky. Heat from his breath, heady with the mixture of alcohol, mingled with her own ragged breath. She'd never had the courage to make the first move, afraid her advances would be rebuffed or worse, afraid she'd be as clumsy in reality as she felt internally. But there was no such fear now.

Lara breathed, then stole the last fraction of an inch.

The kiss trembled on her lips, uncertain, but she moved her mouth against his, only the faintest brush of breath and skin. Will locked his arms around her waist and pulled Lara into arc of his body, molding her against him. He flicked his tongue along the cupid's bow of her lip. Lara opened her mouth, cupped his face in her palms and returned his kiss.

Strong arms tightened and Will tangled one hand in her hair to anchor their bodies together. Lara let the thoughts and regrets and questions seep away on a single breath and found, hiding beneath the uncertainty, a passion that would have frightened her at any other time, with any other man.

From somewhere deep inside, a hot rush of courage welled up and reminded Lara who she'd set out to be before life's expectations had hammered her into someone she didn't recognize.

Her heartbeat thundered in her chest, each breath a roar against her ears. Lara dropped her hands from around his neck, sliding beneath his shirt. She raked her nails down the lines of his shoulders and upper arms, then across his chest. She followed the light matting of honey hair like a blazed trail down the plane of his abs but stopped short of diving into the waistband of his jeans. Instead, she pressed her hand lightly over him through the denim, the material stretched tight over his arousal. Her touch pushed a ragged groan from his throat to rumble against her mouth.

He pulled the hem of her T-shirt from her shorts and Lara didn't protest. Will skimmed his fingers along the bare flesh of her waist, then over her ribs, and Lara didn't protest, but when he cupped her breasts in his palms, caressing her taut nipples with his thumbs, it was Lara's turn to groan.

She didn't wait for reason to cloud out the passion, didn't question the lust burning through her body. For once, Lara followed her heart. She'd let her head deal with things later.

Clothing disappeared as Lara and Will crumbled in a tangle of limbs to the living room carpet. Will braced his body over hers, the tip of his erection brushing against her bare stomach. He parted her legs with his knee, opening her to his heat. Lara grew dizzy, giddy on the combination of alcohol and the brush of Will's hands on her body. She moved her hands over his chest, his shoulders, down the smooth plane of his back. Will mirrored her actions and moved his mouth down the arc of her neck until his tongue teased one erect nipple. Lara gasped and curved into his body.

Will moved his mouth back up to hers and Lara could hear things being moved out of her range of sight. Will rolled to the side and Lara had an instant moment of panic that he'd been the one to come to his senses. Then she heard the crinkle and tear of a cellophane wrapper and realized with embarrassment and relief what he was doing.

Good thing at least one of them could think with more than their libidos.

Will turned back to Lara, curling her into his chest. His face hovered only inches above hers, his breathing as ragged and unsteady as her own. Tiny lines fanned out at the corners of his eyes and mouth. A muscle in his temple twitched. His pulse beat rapidly and thrummed in his neck. The scar beneath his chin had faded and Lara reached up to touch the reminder of their last evening together. Her brother had put that scar there, and then Will had gone away. Forever.

Will waited, studying her as intently as she studied him. She saw him start to open his mouth and knew he would ask if he should stop. Lara silenced his words beneath her mouth and pulled Will to her.

She rose up to meet him and shuddered at the first touch of his body to hers. He moved against her gently, as if afraid she would break. Lara herself wondered if she would shatter. Her body resisted at first. It had been too long, and she sucked in a deep breath as her body sheathed him completely. Will didn't move, feathering kisses across her forehead, down the slope of her neck. He captured her mouth and moved inside her body.

In their union, Lara knew what it was like to be desired and her body responded in kind. She moved against Will with an abandon she didn't know she possessed, knowing for the first time what the articles in Cosmo and Vogue meant. Maybe all the years of sexual dissatisfaction weren't completely her fault.

Their breathing quickened, short, desperate gasps for air and things still out of reach. Lara ran her tongue across Will's bottom lip, startled when he captured it between his teeth, then drew it into his mouth. His tongue played with hers, teasing lightly while his body arched into her. A ribbon of pleasure curled around her insides and Will's eyes fluttered closed as Lara's body tightened around him and shattered into a million pieces. Will stiffened as his release shuddered across the muscles in his back and shoulders, and Lara heard him whisper her name in rush of breath.

Will collapsed against her, his body damp and hot. He smoothed the hair back from her face and kissed her gently, nuzzling her neck and making soft, contented sounds from his throat. He rolled to his back and pulled Lara atop his chest, cradling her head in the hollow of his shoulder.

Lara splayed her fingers across the plane of Will's chest. His heart thundered in unison with hers. As it should be. Karma. Fate. Destiny. Whatever force delivered Will Kenner back to her got a big two thumbs up from Lara.

She stroked his hair, rubbed his temple, and followed the line of his jaw with her finger, touching him in all the ways she'd always wanted to touch him, being bold for the first time in her life. Then Will Kenner did the last thing in the world Lara expected him to do.

He started to snore.

Chapter Five

L ara sat alone in the crowded auditorium. Voices floated above her, bodies moved around her, but she wasn't a part of it. At least she didn't want to be a part of it, because Lara knew without a doubt that she was the topic of conversation in most of the whispering circles huddled around the room.

How long before they all knew that the new Berber carpet hadn't been the only thing to get laid in the living room of the Hastings' place? You didn't have secrets in a small town, at least not for long.

Two days ago, when the coroner came and carried away her dead soon-to-be-ex-husband, Lara sent her pre-planned life with Brian to the morgue as well. All she'd wanted to do was escape the humdrum existence that defined her life, an existence that had been laid out by her family before she knew enough to protest. It strangled her.

Life had never been about choices for the middle daughter of Helen and Howard Caldwell. Lara always knew what was expected of her, knew the role she'd been cast to play in the family drama, and she always received rave reviews because she played her part so well, without requiring a lot of prompting. She was cheerful without being emotional. Enthusiastic without being flamboyant. Giving but never impulsive. Lara always did the right thing because right and wrong were very black and white for a Caldwell.

Then why had life suddenly turned into a thousand shades of grey?

Maybe her world was off balance because she was lost in thoughts of Will and their lovemaking—a word she didn't argue with because no other word would suffice—and the feel of his hands and mouth when she should have been mourning her husband. Lara struggled with that, knowing that a man she hadn't seen in fifteen years could stir more passionate thoughts and emotions—at least until he fell asleep—than her husband of ten years.

She swallowed the tears and screams, but they churned around her insides and scratched at the back of her throat. Besides, Helen Caldwell's daughter would never make a scene in public.

"Lara, honey?"

She cringed inwardly at the familiar voice then felt guilty. Lara loved her mom, she really did, but she wasn't ready to deal with the all-seeing eyes of the woman who could spot an out-of-place hair at thirty paces. Lara pulled up the prom queen smile from the internal safe where she kept all her family-approved responses tucked away.

"Hi, Mom."

Besides, if she was talking with her mother, she wouldn't have to think about the rasp of Will Kenner's five-o'clock shadow burning against her skin. *Men. Can't live with them. Can't run them over with a Buick without raising suspicion.*

"Why are you here, dear? Everyone assumed you'd be at

home." She paused, hunching her body down closer to Lara. "Taking care of *things*." Her mom dropped her voice on the last word to the reverential whisper reserved for distasteful subjects. In the south, if you publicly discussed a distasteful subject in a whisper, it didn't count as gossip.

"*Things,*" Lara whispered too loudly but instantly lowered her voice at her mother's aghast expression, "are on hold for now, Mom. The sheriff isn't releasing the body. Besides, Brian arranged his own funeral years ago. He didn't trust me with the details."

"Speaking of details"—Helen seated herself on the empty chair in front of Lara—"I called your sister and they'll be driving back tonight. They were visiting Jimmy's parents in Gonzales with the kids. Katie's upset you didn't call them yourself."

Lara felt another quick twist of guilt, the emotion more of a family tradition than her grandmother's oyster dressing at Thanksgiving. She'd meant to contact Katie but things had gotten out of control yesterday. She thought of Will. *Way* out of control.

"I'll be sure and apologize to them."

"That's my girl." Helen patted Lara's hand. Then her mom's voice dipped into intervention mode, like someone trying to talk a jumper off the roof of a tall building. "You don't need to be here. You should go home and rest. People are talking. Don't you worry what everyone will—"

"What everyone will think?" Lara finished her mom's sentence before she thought about it. She'd never gone against her mom, not publicly or privately. "This is important," she said, more to herself than her mom. "If the town council approves the construction on that mega store, Belle Terre will never be the same. Gee...run over one dead husband and the whole town starts to talk about you."

Helen stiffened and Lara watched the on-demand tears well up in her eyes. Sometimes Lara thought a last name was the only thing she shared with her mom, but she still felt like a heel for making her mom cry.

"I'm just trying to"—*sniffle*—"look out for you, like I've" —*sniffle*—"always done. Like I've always tried to"—*sniffle*— "look out for this family." Helen pulled a tissue from the pocket of her Halloween sweater.

Lara shrank into her chair. *Frick.*

She was going to hell for making her mom cry. Not the hell that most people thought of when they thought of hell. Not Hell with a capital H, but hell with a lower case h. As in, her mother's *house.* Helen's *house.* Before the carnival tonight, the family would gather, congratulate her brother Paul for his magnificent leadership of the town council, and pretend to be happy about the people they were married to. Like the oyster dressing, it was a family tradition. Lara had counted on using the dead husband excuse to escape tonight's festivities. No such luck.

"Mom, I'm sorry." Lara reached out and put her hand on her mother's shoulder as the woman hiccupped through her tears and dabbed carefully at the tears that hadn't fallen. "It's just that...well..."

Why didn't she just tell her mom why stopping this store was so important to her? She was going to lose her book-store, the one thing in life she'd accomplished on her own and the one thing she'd kept a complete and total secret from her family, even to the point of hiring someone to pay the mortgage each month. It had taken every penny she had, which was why she couldn't move out when she asked for the divorce.

She owned the store, but the property was a joint venture, and that was the problem she had to face now. As it stood, she was the only voice of dissent keeping LCB Construction from building a mega store. She'd dug a hole so deep with the secrets, afraid to rock the leaking boat of her family, that she didn't know if she could find the shore again.

Lara sighed inwardly and plastered on her fake smile until her cheeks hurt. "Never mind. I'm just not myself today."

Helen sniffled and smiled, the brimming tears vanishing in a single breath. "No one expects you to be yourself, dear."

Truer words had never been spoken and they echoed in Lara's head. Could she merge the expectations of her family with the reality of what she wanted? Would they allow it? Heck, Lara chided herself. She was a grown woman! Why did she need their permission? It wasn't a need, Lara admitted, but it would be nice to have someone accept her for who she was. Helen pushed to her feet and joined a group of ladies watching them from a few feet away.

She doubted little much could top the week she'd had so far.

Pay the electric bill. Check.

Run over dead husband. Check.

Make mother cry. Check.

Have sex with new neighbor. Check.

That last one might deserve a double check, although Will didn't necessarily qualify as a "new" neighbor. He'd grown up in Belle Terre, on the other side of the proverbial tracks, but Will had been her brother's best friend. Then Will was sent away one awful, wonderful night, and none of their lives were ever the same. Maybe that was why she'd always done what people expected. The one night she'd done what she'd wanted, someone had paid too high a price for her rebelliousness.

Lara straightened her back and tucked her legs beneath the chair, certain no one would bother her after her mother's tearful breakdown. She caught snatches of conversation about the "stiff" but pushed the buzz to the back of her mind.

After her adventure on the new Berber carpet yesterday, Lara had walked calmly and carefully across the street back to her house. After re-planting her camellia—it was Thursday, after all—she'd stood under a hot shower and tried to cry away her lust for a man she'd always wanted but had never been brave enough to go after. Could she pretend that it meant nothing to her, as it meant to him? Even beneath the spray of the hot shower, she could smell the scent of Will's body on her own. Lara had wanted to rub it into her flesh rather than brush it away.

But her worst fears came true. Rather than stir Will's passions, she bored him to sleep. Maybe Brian's indiscretions had been her fault. She'd bored him and he'd gone looking to other women. Five other women at last count, to be exact. She'd suspected two years ago after she'd gone to the bank for a loan to buy the bookstore. She'd over heard the loan officer, a Clairol-redhead with some double-D perkiness parked on her chest, talking with another bank employee. Apparently you could keep some secrets in a small town.

She didn't confront him about it. He'd have denied it and she didn't have proof. Then, yesterday, she'd gone through Brian's things at home, and between his three cell phones Lara discovered a few hundred sext messages that would make even Angelina Williams blush. His taste apparently ran to women who, like his wife and her Welcome Wagon platter and pitcher, could help his business—the bank loan officer, the mayor's personal assistant, the city treasurer, the community development commissioner, and the only female police officer in town—who'd cried all over the crime scene and had to be sent away by the sheriff though Lara didn't know why at the time. There wasn't an office in town that Brian wasn't plugged into. Literally.

She didn't even get the satisfaction of confronting him on his affairs. Brian went and died on her. The jerk.

Maybe she could be a nun. Could nuns own bookstores? Lara doubted it, and they sure couldn't sleep with sexy bad boys who moved in across the street.

Not that she'd ever sleep with him again. The jerk. But maybe there'd be another sexy bad boy in her future. Someone who'd fight for the girl and sacrifice his own wants and needs. Someone worthy of the Angelina Williams title of hero.

As if summoned by her thoughts, Lara watched Will slip into the auditorium and prop himself up against the back wall. He kept his gaze over the crowd, not meeting the two hundred or so pairs of eyes that bore into him as if he were the last piece of Mrs. Farmer's Better than Sex pound cake. His body seemed tense, wide shoulders tight beneath the tailored jacket. The black T-shirt tucked into his jeans rode his torso as he drew a breath and highlighted the hard lines of his ribs.

Lickable. That was the word that came to mind when Lara looked at Will. Lickable from head to toe...with a few detours in between, of course. She rubbed the pounding headache in her temple. She apparently possessed nothing worthy of a detour. She hadn't been able to satisfy Brian. Why did she think she could satisfy any man?

Maybe being what everyone expected wasn't so bad, Lara reasoned. Whatever else her family was, they were hers, and maybe it was selfish to change the rules at this point.

But it was her life! She deserved some happiness, too. Didn't she?

She hoped for the space of one heartbeat that Will had come to find her and apologize for falling asleep, and the lust that Lara tried to wash away yesterday in the shower surfaced once again. But he just stood there, face concentrated into blankness while he watched the town council file onto the makeshift stage. She was being selfish. Worse, she was being foolish. Wanting what you couldn't have just caused heartache. She knew that better than anyone.

Paul Caldwell, town mayor and Lara's older brother, took the podium. He shuffled around a handful of papers and Lara didn't think she'd ever seen her brother look so unprepared. For Paul, preparation wasn't just a choice. It was a way of life. But tonight, his tie hung crooked, revealing a coffee stain on his rumpled shirt. Either Paul was learning to relax or he'd hit a few bumps in his idyllic road of life. Lara sympathized. She'd found a few speed bumps lately as well.

The mayor looked up from his preparations from the meeting and Lara saw his gaze immediately find Will in the back of the audience. Paul clutched the podium briefly, then left the stage and headed toward Will.

Will's face remained blank, but he spread his legs and folded his arms across his chest as if preparing for an assault, stretching his body to its full six feet. Lara hadn't seen Will look so closed-off since their last night together fifteen years ago. Paul approached cautiously and held out his hand. The two exchanged a few words before Will accepted Paul's handshake with a weak smile. Lara could sense the ancient shadow of animosity between the two former friends, and the old regret over Will's last night in town bubbled up inside of her.

Paul returned to the stage and the crowd shuffled to their seats, the hum of voices fading into the rafters. Lara could hold onto the luxury of denial about Will for a few more hours.

Paul tapped the microphone. The feedback wailed into the audience and the room quieted immediately. Nothing like a punctured eardrum to silence a crowd.

"Ladies and gentlemen, while Sally passes out the meeting agenda, I wanted to go over a few things."

Sally Caldwell, Paul's wife and council secretary, huffed from her chair and began distributing the aforementioned agendas. She didn't look happy. Sally was always happy in that June Cleaver-slash-Norman Bates sort of way. Sally and Paul had the American dream all wrapped up in a three-bedroom ranch house on Walnut Street. Four kids. Two cars. Satellite dish on the front lawn. They were a made-for-TV movie waiting to happen.

Paul *ahem*ed in the microphone again and Lara turned off the mental tabloid headlines flashing through her mind. She'd run over her dead husband two days ago on her way to visit a bookstore she pretended not to own.

Who was she to cast stones?

Chapter Six

Will could not believe Paul approached him in front of a room full of people, and feared he was going to apologize for the last moments of their friendship those many years ago. The apology wasn't necessary, at least not in Will's mind, and he was glad when Paul just shook his hand and welcomed him back to town. Will had made his own choice that night and in doing so, perhaps saved two futures, Paul's and his own. Now, with his future riding on the outcome of this town meeting, Will wondered if returning to Belle Terre had been the right decision.

And now there was Lara to consider. He wanted to kick himself for letting things go so far with her, but damn, he'd wanted her for so long. Will loved Lara Caldwell in high school but could never have given her what she deserved back then. Seeing her yesterday not only got his libido going, but kick-started his heart. He'd not felt like that for anyone, sadly, not even for the woman he'd married. His ex had known it, too, and told him when she left that if he was going to find happiness, he'd have to find Lara again. That was three years ago. He'd been looking for a chance to get back to Belle Terre since then.

But he'd screwed it up. After fifteen years of waiting for a second chance, and three years of working toward making that chance a reality, when he finally had the woman of his dreams in his arms, and naked to boot, he'd fallen asleep. The rumble of regret growled from his throat.

Impulse. He'd acted without thinking things through, something he'd promised never to do again. It was something the old Will would have done and he had learned early the consequences of rash actions. His old man taught him well. So had Paul Caldwell. Will traced the ridge of scar tissue beneath his lower lip, his constant reminder of Lara since he'd left Belle Terre.

Will sucked in a breath and let it out slowly, finding his center, that place within himself where he'd gone so many times when he was a kid. He pushed down the emotion because he had other things to focus on. There were people counting on him. And he couldn't, *wouldn't* let them down.

At least he'd fallen asleep *after* they'd made love, he consoled himself.

When he'd regained consciousness a few hours later, she'd already gone. He could still feel her moving beneath him, still smell her on his skin. The sweetness of her kiss, so gentle and hesitant, as if she waited for him to tell her she was doing it right. Lara made him feel things he'd forgotten and shoved aside, things that hadn't fit into his life after he'd left. She'd stolen his heart when they were kids and he'd touched a part of her soul that she'd never allowed to be free.

Will had lain on the carpet and mentally shaken himself. Lara was vulnerable. He could see it in the tight line of her shoulders and the crinkle of tension knotted in her brow, but he sensed the passion waiting for release when he'd kissed her, the same passion she'd held in check when they were kids.

Returning to Belle Terre, even temporarily, would be difficult, too many old ghosts waiting to raise up when he least expected. He thought he'd rid himself of the images from his childhood when he left town. Only Will didn't leave town. He was sent away.

But being sent away was probably one of the best things that could have happened to the seventeen-year-old would-be juvenile delinquent. He'd escaped the expectations of the town. They weren't the same expectations that most young men were saddled with at that age. Not college and career and marriage and family. Everyone expected him to turn out like his old man, a drunk, or his brother, a convicted thief. His sister had faced the same struggles—like mother, like daughter. She'd been looking for love in all the wrong places since she'd been old enough to sneak into the wrong places.

Belle Terre had not been kind to the Kenner children. Lara and Paul had tried to change that, but they'd been trapped by their own burden of expectations, and in the end, it was those expectations that cost Will what he wanted more than anything in this world. A home.

He sighed inwardly and thought of all the things a successful project here would get him. Security with future contracts and a steady income. Success. The self-satisfaction of knowing that, though he hadn't done it completely on his own, he'd done it nonetheless. He'd be leaving in six months, just long enough to get the AmeriMart project completed and show Belle Terre, and Lara, that he'd made good. Maybe she'd even come with him.

Will gazed out over people he'd known since childhood.

Would they give him a second chance? Could they let go of the memory of his family and the trouble they'd caused for so long?

In the corner of the room opposite from Will, a young boy stood quietly apart from the crowd. Will took in the ill-fitting clothes and guessed his age to be about twelve or thirteen, but the distrust in his wary stance added to the years.

Will let his attention from the young boy drift as Paul Caldwell called the meeting to order. The council moved quickly through the agenda and Will's attention narrowed as they moved to new business.

"The council will now hear opinions regarding the pending approval of the permit for LCB Construction to build on the land adjacent to the southwest perimeter of Rochelle Park."

A woman began making her way across the gymnasium as Paul introduced the item. The woman walked in short-steps to the microphone, her blonde head wobbling like a bobblehead doll. She wore a white sweatshirt with a blue fish emblazoned across her ample chest, the letters C.O.D. printed in the fish's body.

"Candace Barr, your honor, speaking on behalf of the Coalition for Order and Decency." She traced her fingers over the fish emblem when she said the name of the group.

Will heard more than one exasperated sigh escape from the people closest to him. He noticed a few other women in the audience with matching sweatshirts. Candace patted her hair and straightened her skirt while the noise subsided, and the attention returned to her.

"I'd like to propose that the first item on the agenda be changed. The Coalition for Order and Decency demands that the council put an ordinance in place regarding the por-nog-raphy Mr. Lautner displays at The Book Nook.

Those *books* send the wrong message to visitors. My fellow coalition members agree that abomination needs to go!"

A spattering of applause rippled through the audience, but Candace and her coalition didn't appear to have strong support. Will eye's returned to Lara, sitting nearest to Candace. He thought she was going to shoot out of her chair and throttle the woman if the deep splotches of red slashing up her neck and into her cheeks were any indication of her inner feelings.

Paul half-stood to address the speaker, his body language saying he knew how this would end. "There's a motion on the floor. Do I hear a second?"

"I second," a shaky voice intoned from the depths of the audience.

Still leaning over the microphone, Paul announced, "We have a motion that has been moved and seconded. All in favor please say aye."

A few ayes rose from the crowd.

"All opposed?"

They gym resounded with the nays and Paul shrugged his shoulders at Candace. "The motion has been defeated."

But Candace wouldn't give up the floor. She pumped her meaty fist in the air. "We demand action, Mr. Mayor."

Paul again half rose from his chair. "You're very aware of the procedures to put a proposition before the board, Mrs. Barr. This council has entertained your ordinance no fewer than four times over the course of the last year. Also, if the first item on the agenda is passed, your motion will become moot as the bookstore will no longer be in operation. Now I'd like to keep this meeting going so we can all get to the street fair on time."

A stronger ovation arose at Paul's statement and Candace retreated to her seat, but not before her eyes met

Lara's and the two seem to exchange a silent declaration of war. Will would have to remember to ask Lara about that. If she ever spoke to him again.

Paul pushed his papers aside and adjusted the microphone. "Back to the first item of business. I'd like to be the first to speak on this issue, if no one objects." Paul scanned the room, then looked back at the council members, but no objections were voiced. "We've all been tightening out belts for years now as the economy of this area has moved out or been taken out by one disaster or another, but we've survived because we've stuck together."

Applause followed Paul's words.

"We have to do that now. This superstore will create economic security for the people of Belle Terre. It will create new jobs and bring in new customers for our existing businesses. We will see an influx of new neighbors. The benefits of allowing this construction are numerous and I urge the council to approve this permit. New business is the lifeblood of a community."

Thunderous applause echoed against the metal walls of the gym. Will found his attention immediately centered on Lara, but she sat quietly in her chair, her hands clasped in her lap. New business. New jobs. What could she have against economic security?

Will watched his former Social Studies teacher approach the microphone. Will smiled. Mr. Henley still had a fondness for ugly bow ties and comb-overs. Did he have the same penchant for fairness?

"This superstore will bring a lot of business from outside of Belle Terre, that's true. That's always good for a town." Henley pulled on his bow tie thoughtfully for a moment. "But it will also change the town. Now, will the change be for the better or the worse? Are we a town that prefers the new over the old? That's what the mayor and town council, in truth, what everyone here needs to decide."

Mr. Henley took his seat in the front row and Will watched a few more people file up to the microphone. Most were in favor of the vote. Some seemed as neutral as Mr. Henley. Others brought in issues as varied as the people presenting them. Some tree-huggers were concerned about a dead one-hundred-year-old cedar and another group reported the possible existence of a white-tailed dwarf titmouse.

But it wasn't until Lara rose from her chair that Will got the sense his first real opposition was about to speak, and for reasons he didn't try to analyze, he wanted her approval more than anything.

"The superstore will destroy this town." Lara's voice cracked over the microphone. Her fists remained stiffly clenched at her side, making dents in the fabric of her skirt, but the determined set of her chin told Will that this fight was about more than just the town. Lara was taking this extremely personally, and personal was something he understood on this project.

Voices buzzed and the hum of tension crackled through the gymnasium. Helen Caldwell rose from her seat and started toward Lara, but Lara narrowed her eyes at her mother and Helen chose a quiet retreat. *Smart lady.*

Lara's brother stepped up to the microphone. "Lara, I think you're overreacting a bit. Perhaps, given the events of this week you have—"

Lara pulled herself straight and swiped back a wayward curl. "Don't patronize me, Paul. I may be your sister, but here in this gymnasium I'm a voting member of this community."

The collective hive buzzed behind Lara, some nodding

their heads in support, others shaking their heads in shock. Will heard one or two whisper that Lara must be "beside herself with grief." Quite the contrary, Will thought. He'd never seen Lara more sure of herself.

"My apologies, Mrs. Haley," he gritted out coldly, enunciating her name sharply. "Please continue."

Will watched Lara deflate a bit and could see the hesitation flicker across her face. Lara looked up and found him with her eyes. Did the use of her married name trigger some memory? Was she thinking of their lovemaking with regret?

Will knew Lara had a strong sense of duty to family. He'd seen the distress when she was faced with choosing between what she wanted and what her family wanted. Going against her brother, especially in a public forum, went against Lara's very nature. What could mean so much to her that she'd go against her family?

"The mayor is correct. This superstore will create economic security, but only for LCB Construction and the bigwigs sitting behind their desks a thousand miles away in Chicago. It will displace businesses that have been in place in this community for more than three generations. It will put people out of work."

Another member of the council took the microphone. "I disagree, Lara. The superstore will create two new jobs for every one that is displaced."

A few voices of approval sounded out. Will could tell Lara was struggling to remain stoic, but her clenched fists had started to shake with the contained tension.

"Two minimum-wage jobs," Lara added quickly. "The management jobs will be held by outsiders brought in by AmeriMart, not by the members of our community."

A third member of the council rose to her feet but did not take the microphone. "Since the Piggly Wiggly closed, we have to drive to Donnelly for groceries. What about the new customers that will come to Belle Terre for the super-store and will spend their money in our other businesses?"

Lara turned to the audience, searching the crowd. She pointed to a woman in the back. "Mrs. Jackson. You own the pharmacy. Do you think you can compete with the corpo-rate buying power of AmeriMart?" She pointed to a gentleman sitting just a few seats away. "What about the butcher shop, Mr. Lutz? Can you compete with their prices?"

Mrs. Jackson and Mr. Lutz remained quiet, but Will could tell Lara was asking questions either no one had thought of, or no one had had the courage to ask.

"It will only be a matter of time, and one by one we'll lose the very people that made Belle Terre what it is. Those bigwigs don't care about this community. LCB Construction doesn't care about this community."

Will watched the change in the crowd. For someone so unsure of herself, Lara was proving a powerful speaker.

Another gentleman from the audience took the micro-phone. He introduced himself as Walton McCoy and Will recognized the name as one of the business owners who'd agreed to sell. "The bookstore is the single holdout. What about the other owners that have decided to sell? When is the owner going to come forward and meet us face-to-face to discuss the sale?"

The audience buzzed as Mr. McVoy made his way back to his chair. Lara looked to someone in the audience, then again faced the microphone. "I–I won't speak for the book-store owner," she said. "I just want to encourage the city council to consider what will happen to this town by letting outsiders bring in the AmeriMart store."

Paul Caldwell again took the podium with a white-knuckled grip on his temper. "But it's one of our very own that brings us this golden opportunity, Lara. Will Kenner." Paul pointed toward Will, and Will froze as if caught in a tractor beam. "Will will oversee the construction of the AmeriMart in Belle Terre."

Like birds in flight, every head swiveled to follow Paul's finger and two hundred pairs of eyes lay to rest on Will. But it was only Lara's eyes that Will cared about. And hers were filling with anger and tears.

Chapter Seven

Will walked slowly through the center aisle, mounting the steps of the raised platform with the weight of certain doom pressing on his shoulders. Paul motioned for Will to approach the microphone and Will joined him reluctantly. The mayor extended his hand to Will.

"Thank you, Paul." Will thought of the welcome he'd gotten from Lara and wanted nothing more than to jump down from the platform, sweep her into his arms and back to his house. Judging from the look he'd gotten just a few moments ago, she'd put up more of a fight this time.

The world narrowed. The intensity of her gaze sizzled along his flesh as strongly as the memory of her kiss. There was so much he wanted to ask her, so much he wanted to explain.

"Well la-dee-friggin'-da." The drunken voice rose up from the crowd and Will caught the first glimpse of his sister in nearly fifteen years. She pushed to her feet unsteadily. "The long-lost son returns."

Will flashed back to so many moments in his life—his first day of kindergarten, the first little league game when he was seven, the Christmas pageant when he was eight. By the time Will turned nine, he knew better than to be anywhere public where his family might show up.

Chloe had turned into their mother, from the blackened roots of her blonde hair to the too-small clothes hugging her rail-thin body.

"Guess you got what you wanted, Willy-boy. The town's finally glad to have you here, but you're still Royal Kenner's kid." She lit a cigarette and motioned to the podium with the fire-red tip. "And that one is just as likely to—"

"Enough, Chloe." Will stepped down from the podium and made his way through the crowd to his sister. He ignored the openmouthed stares and reproachful looks coming from the audience. He'd been fighting against the judgment coming at him now his whole life. Taking her by the arm, he led his sister from the auditorium. She stumbled in the spike heels more than once during the short walk, dropping her still-lit cigarette, but they were able to get outside without any major catastrophe.

Jasmine and sweet olive swirled through the night air and the evening sky was as clear as Will remembered, a perfect backdrop of deepening shades of blue pinpricked with light. The moon, with its crisp, clean edges, looked like a cutout against the darkness.

Even though Chloe had been the older sister, Will had always been the one to take care of her. Within a few weeks of his arrest and departure from Belle Terre, he learned she'd found her own escape and married the first of three losers, each a replica of their drunken father. Maybe the Kenners weren't meant to find happiness. Will sighed.

"Don't you be giving me none of your high-and-mighty attitude, Willy-boy. You ain't no better'n me." A strand of over-bleached, over-permed hair fell across Chloe's face and she shoved it back behind her ear. She retrieved a pack of Marlboros from her purse, but the breeze and her trembling hands wouldn't let her light the cigarette.

"I never thought I was better than you, Chloe." The monotone of his voice sounded sharper than he intended and he watched Chloe stiffen, albeit unsteadily. Will took the lighter gently from her and cupped his hand around the flame, then waited while she sucked the cigarette to life. "And please don't call me Willy-boy."

She saluted sharply. "Yessir, Mr. Kenner, sir." A twin jet-stream of smoke exhaled from her nostrils.

"Cut it out, Chloe." Will reached over and clasped her hand to lower it. Her wrists were slender, fragile, but nothing in the deep lines framing her mouth and eyes indicated frailty. The realization jabbed at Will. He pulled her carefully toward the wooden bench under the walkway and they sat.

He barely knew where to begin. Will thought he'd prepared for this, thought he'd been ready to deal with the ghosts of his past. Returning to Belle Terre, even though he was no longer the same kid, wasn't going to be easy.

"I know you're mad at me. You have a right to be."

Though his exit from Belle Terre hadn't been his doing, he'd taken the out and had been relieved to leave behind the shadow of his family. He'd built a new life and abandoned the old.

"I haven't been here for the family like I should have."

"Ha." Chloe's face slackened, then a wariness that looked too familiar resettled deep in her eyes. "Fat lotta good that does. 'Sides, you're more interested in Miss Priss than any *family* you might have. I remember what her family did to you, even if you don't."

The ache caught him unaware, and the mixture of regret and anger squeezed his gut. On what turned out to be his last night in town, Lara and he had taken his bike for a ride. He'd felt her arms around his middle, her hands buried in the pockets of his leather jacket, her chin resting on his shoulder. Not even the air speeding by their faces could carry away the scent of her, a swirl of lemon and flowers he couldn't name. When they'd arrived at the lake, Paul had been furious.

He shook away the memory and shifted uncomfortably. "I remember what happened, Chloe, but don't blame Lara." Will looked back to the gym, wishing he could see through the doors to the interior where Lara sat.

Chloe snorted, flicking the cigarette ash expertly from the red tip. "You ever tell her the truth about that night? You ever tell anyone?"

"What good would it have done?"

Chloe gestured toward the gym. "Don't you think the good people of Belle Terre should know the truth about the mayor? Or is the truth just for other folks and not the Caldwells?"

Will shook his head. "They're just as much prisoners of their family as we were of ours."

"And you think you can change that? You gonna save her, too?"

Chloe watched him with an intensity he couldn't bear, her eyes so much like their mother's he was caught off guard by memories sharp enough to sting.

"I learned my lesson long ago, Chloe," he admitted reluctantly. "I didn't come back to save anyone. I just hoped I could...help."

Silence swelled between them for a few moments. Chloe puffed heavily on the burning cigarette and released another acrid stream of smoke on a heavy release of breath. Will stretched out his legs, resting one ankle on top of the other, palms pressed flat against the bench.

"How's the house holding up?" he asked finally, trying for a safer topic than his failure as a brother. Chloe still lived in the house where they grew up, returning after the end of her last marriage to the only place either could ever call home.

She nodded. "It's okay. After Dad died, a man came by and gave us a check. Said it was insurance money and I was the beneficiary."

Will kept his gaze down. "Oh?"

"Yeah. It paid for some repairs we needed. New roof. AC. New appliances for the kitchen." Chloe hesitated as her voice trembled, examining a broken nail with more attention than it needed. "Guess it was lucky Dad had that policy."

"Yeah, I guess it was." Will shrugged out of his jacket and draped it over his sister's shoulders. "You ever see Junior?" The oldest of the three kids, Royal Jr., had gone to jail on Will's fifteenth birthday, though Will had never known why. Will almost followed his lead two years later but had luckily been treated as a first-time juvenile offender thanks to the sheriff's intervention. Without that, Will didn't know where he'd be today.

"Junior's up for parole soon," Chloe said on a rush of breath as she exhaled more smoke. "You gonna try and save him, too, while you're in town?"

Before Will could answer, Chloe waved him away with a swipe of her hand. His dad's rattletrap '92 LeBaron pulled into the circular drive and idled noisily, the exterior now more rust than red paint. The driver hunkered down behind the steering wheel, perhaps to lessen the chance of recognition, but Will realized he was the same boy as the one he'd seen inside the auditorium. It might be the closest he got to meeting his nephew.

"My ride is here." Chloe puffed once more on the Marlboro, then crushed it out beneath the toe of her shoe. She pitched his coat back at him. "I won't be expecting no invitation to Thanksgiving dinner."

When she rose to her feet, Chloe swayed with the effort. Will offered his arm, but she slapped it away and dropped his coat into his lap. She staggered toward the waiting car.

The rejection stung, but Will knew he deserved it. "Let me come to the house. Meet..." Will choked on the realization that he couldn't remember the names of his niece and nephew. "Let me meet your kids. I want to help." Even to him, the offer sounded weak. Maybe coming back here had been a mistake. He'd turned out no better than his old man, ignoring his family, forcing them to fend for themselves.

"You send your help every month." His sister paused but did not turn around. Her shoulders shook a little, as if the emotions vibrated beneath her skin. Chloe wrenched open the door and held onto it for balance. "You couldn't save us when we was kids, Will. What makes you think you can save us now?"

His sister slid into the front seat of the rattletrap and slammed the door shut. Maybe she wanted to shut out Will as well.

Her words echoed his last meeting with Lara.

"But Will, I have to do something." Lara sobbed, each tear *wearing away another corner of Will's heart.*

"You can't save me, Lara. Don't even try."

Will returned to Belle Terre to show the only people

whose opinion he cared about that he'd made something of himself. For the first time, he questioned the rationale in that decision. Maybe it would have been easier elsewhere, someplace where the memories didn't haunt him at every turn. Junior had been lost for so long Will hadn't spared a thought for him in more than a decade. He'd virtually turned his back on Chloe, leaving her on her own. Maybe Chloe was right. Maybe the Kenner kids weren't worth saving.

But even if there was no salvation for the Kenner family, there were people out there counting on him and Will didn't want to let them down. People had put their faith in the reputation of LCB Construction, had put their money on *him*, Will Kenner. Lara had always believed in him when they were kids, and he wanted to show her that her faith had been worthwhile.

People started to file out of the auditorium, but if a decision had been reached, it was not evident on their faces. Will searched the departing crowd for Lara but did not see her emerge, so he shrugged into his jacket and weaved his way back inside.

Lara still sat in her chair, legs properly crossed at the ankles beneath the skirt of her dark green dress. She tugged the edges of a white sweater tightly across her chest, one arm hugging her waist. If he didn't see her chewing absently on her fingernail, he would have thought her to be as inwardly calm as she appeared outwardly, but Will knew better.

Lara was a worrier. Always had been. She wanted to fit into the mold carved out by her family and friends, but he sensed in her the same desire to escape the expectations of others, and it looked like her square corners were finally pressing against the rounded edges of the life that had been defined for her. If she only believed in herself as much as Will believed in her.

She'd had a tough couple of days and Will felt certain he didn't know the half of it as of yet. Running over your dead almost ex-husband had to be traumatic. Not to mention his own contribution to her crappy day. But Will didn't think he was the basis for the lost look in Lara's eyes when it was announced that he was heading up the construction on the AmeriMart, and if she knew the truth... Will didn't want to think what look would be in her eyes then.

She'd loved the town when they were growing up and wanted to preserve the Mayberry-esque quality for her own children, but Will didn't think Lara had children, and that was something else he wondered about. She adored kids and had planned on having a large family. Why had her plans changed? Or had someone changed them for her?

Will cut a broad path through the room and approached Lara. He turned one of the folding chairs around and straddled it, crossing his arms across the back.

"Maybe we should talk."

"Kind of late for pillow talk, don't you think? But wait...if you really want to..." Lara scooted her body down the chair, closed her eyes, and rested her chin against her shoulder. Then she feigned a light snore. Will wanted to laugh but figured Lara was entitled to some righteous indignation. He deserved it. Besides, it brought a little color back to her cheeks.

Hands lifted in surrender, Will acquiesced. "All right, all right. I'm a bastard."

Lara raised her head and quirked one eyebrow in his direction. That troublesome curl lollygagged over her left eye, but she didn't brush it away. "A rat bastard."

"OK. A rat bastard. But I did drive a thousand miles to get here for this meeting tonight. Please forgive me."

"I don't know." A smile teased the corner of her mouth, but it warred with something deeper inside and disappeared.

"And I'm a snake."

She bit her lip and Will had to remind himself to concentrate on groveling for forgiveness when he really wanted to lean forward and kiss her. "Am I forgiven?"

Lara sat up a little straighter and folded her arms across her chest. "Maybe."

"I don't regret what happened yesterday."

Lara felt the blood rush to her toes, then explode upward to her face as if propelled by volcanic forces. She reminded herself to breathe, to blink, to close her mouth so her tonsils didn't dry out.

"And I know you probably do, and that's okay," Will interrupted the churning of her brain. "It was unexpected. It was probably not the brightest move for either of us. But I still don't regret it. I came back here because of you, Lara. Because there were so many things left unfinished last time I left town. I'm not going to let that happen this time."

"Will..." *Breathe. Blink. Close your mouth.* The quiet little voice inside Lara's head, the one that told her not to marry Brian Haley, the one that told her to proclaim her ownership of The Book Nook, started screaming *Shut up and kiss him*.

Instead, Lara sprang to her feet and sought the nearest escape. Her sensible flats slapped across the hard gym floor, each staccato step in rhythm to her palpitating heart. Not even the flowing fabric of her dress could keep up with her and fanned out behind her like the wake of a speeding boat.

It was just too much for Lara to deal with. She'd spent

three years grieving for a marriage that her husband didn't care about. Lara had let him ignore her. Lara had let herself believe it would all get better, even when it didn't.

But everyone expected her to be the grieving widow and Lara always lived up to people's expectations. She didn't know how to let people down. She'd never failed at being the respectable daughter or wife because she'd never been allowed to fail.

A set of footsteps echoed Lara's as she crossed the gymnasium floor and she remembered the last time he'd followed her.

"You can't come with me, Lara."

"Why not? Because of my parents? I'm eighteen. I can do what I want."

"You would never hurt your family, and even if you would, I wouldn't let you. Not for me."

"I didn't come back to town to hurt you." Will's voice wrapped around Lara's heart and squeezed.

Lara stopped and whirled around so fast Will nearly collided with her. "Why are you back?"

"That's one of the things we need to talk about. You always had faith in me when we were kids." He reached out toward her but she shied away, not knowing if she could bear his touch. A wounded look crossed behind his eyes and she regretted putting it there. "I want you to know that kept me going."

She closed her eyes and rubbed at the tightness over the bridge of her nose. When she opened her eyes to look at him again, a familiar pain stabbed at her gut. "And to repay me you, what, thought I needed an AmeriMart store?" Lara again turned and continued walking toward the exit. "Whatever happened yesterday...with us...whatever that was...it's just not the right time."

"It was never the right time, Lara." He exhaled slowly, dropping his shoulders. "I didn't expect this, but now that it's happened...I'm going to be here for six months if the building permit is approved. Can we just try this time? I don't care what other people think."

"I have to care, Will. I live here. I'm not just passing through. This is my home. These are my neighbors, my friends, my *family*." The first tears rose in Lara's eyes, pushed upward by the growing lump in her throat.

Will claimed the last few inches separating the two of them and Lara's body hummed with the nearness of his body. The familiar scents of soap and pinewood circled around him and she breathed in the memory of his skin against hers.

"I worked hard to get here today." Lara could see the struggle written in his eyes. "I won't just walk away. But I've always cared for you."

"Why?" She stiffened and drew back her shoulders, but Lara's empty heart pulled the pride from her stance. Then the words rushed out before she could stop them. "Do you need someone to serve on the welcoming committee because no one else will do it? Do you need me to hand out fliers for your campaign? Do you need me to babysit because I don't have any kids, so obviously I have nothing else to do on a Saturday night? Do you need someone to look good on your arm so people think you're a family man? Do you need a champion for your AmeriMart project? What do you want from me, Will? Because everyone wants something that I can't...*won't*... give anymore."

Will opened his mouth to speak, shut it, then started again. "This store means a lot to me, but so do you. We had something when we were kids. I want to find the Lara that was taken from me. I think she's still in there, and that's who I want."

Lara shook her hair back and tried to appear casual. "Well, you had me. I hope it was worth the trip."

But Will had found the one place in her heart still weak and alone, the place that still wanted someone to love her for no other reason than because she was Lara.

Chapter Eight

L ara stared at the empty chair across from her at her parents' table for eight. Before Brian had died, they'd filled the antique table perfectly for each holiday or family dinner. The Caldwell children on one side. Their respective spouses on the other. The kids nearby at the table in the kitchen. A parent at each end, perfect bookends to the perfect family. Now Brian's chair sat empty, and as the assorted vegetables, dinner rolls, and snarky comments went round the table, it didn't feel quite so perfect.

"I really don't know why you didn't ask me about this, Paul," Sally uttered disdainfully, plopping a spoonful of mashed potatoes on her plate before a voice whined out "Mom!" and she went to check on the kids in the kitchen. She was a chorus of perfectly matched perfection, from her navy pinstripe sweater dress to the identical headband holding back her Hollywood-chic haircut.

"We've done Christmas cards every year since I've been mayor, Sally!" Paul yelled to his departing wife as he accepted the green beans. "Why should this year be any different?"

"Because *we* don't do the cards. *I* do the cards," she explained, returning to the table. "And now that *you're* running for state senate, you'll make the list even bigger. Maybe I have other things to do."

Paul huffed. "What do you have to do?" he asked innocently and Lara cringed inwardly for her clueless brother.

Katie, Lara and Paul's younger sister, chimed in as she went to check on her own children. "Yeah, Paul. Why not get one of your campaign workers to do them?"

As Lara's eyes went from Paul to Katie, she realized how much the two of them looked like their mother—hair the color of a café au lait, vivid blue eyes in a triangular-shaped face—while she looked more like their father, green eyes in a round face surrounded by a head full of cherry-cola hair.

"Because he doesn't have any campaign workers. He has me. And I don't get paid, not even in thank-yous." Sally sniffled as she sat back down at the dining room and Lara watched her sister-in-law's eyes fill with tears.

Jimmy, Katie's husband, nudged his wife with his elbow when she returned to the table moment later. "See there, sweetheart, Sally works for Paul and doesn't expect to get paid."

Another chorus of "Mom!" came from the kitchen and Katie tossed her napkin on the table. "I already work for a living raising your four children. If you want help in the store, hire some damn help," Katie snapped and glared at Jimmy. Jimmy wisely went back to his ham and potatoes as his wife stalked off to the kitchen.

"He thinks he doesn't have to pay me," Sally ground out, wiping her eyes with her napkin. "Something else he hasn't consulted me on since all this mayor nonsense started twelve years ago." A call of "Mom!" from the kitchen had Sally jumping up again.

Lara passed the next set of dishes around, realizing she had nothing on her plate. Grabbing the platter of ham from the center of the table, she slid a piece onto her plate. Paul had run for mayor at Brian's urging over a dinner very much like this one, she remembered. They'd only been dating at the time. Brian had already graduated from college and made himself part of the family since his own parents' deaths. Looking back, Lara was sure Brian had calculated the influence he could wring out of being brothers-in-law with the mayor. Even with family, Brian sought out personal advantages. As this thought played out in her head, Lara realized she'd transferred practically all of the glazed ham onto her plate, so she returned the near-empty platter to the table. No one else seemed to notice.

"Now Sally," Helen interjected sweetly as her daughter-in-law passed her chair once again. "Paul is going to be an excellent state senator. We're all going to be there tonight to help him. My Tuesday bridge partner, Susan Kimball, is going to watch the kids, and think how wonderful it will be for you as a state senator's wife."

"Helen," Lara's father warned softly. "Let Sally and Paul work out their own marital issues."

Helen narrowed her gaze on her husband through the carefully arranged centerpiece of hibiscus that Lara was certain came from her own backyard. "Anything at this table is family business, Howard."

Sally rejoined the table once again. Lara had never seen her parents share a cross word with each other. Of course, she realized, she'd never seen them share a kiss, either. Was her family crumbling before her, or had it always been a little dented and broken?

"The only family business we need to be discussing tonight is Lara," Howard reminded them.

And collectively the entire table focused their attention on Lara and her untouched plate of ham. "What?" she questioned, feeling like the dream of going to school naked was coming true at her parents' dinner table.

"We're worried about you, sis," Katie said as she returned to the table, putting her hand on Lara's shoulder. Only two years younger than her, Katie had done the dutiful wife thing in her seven-year marriage and produced two sets of twins, the identical girls now five and identical boys now three. They did keep her busy.

The sound of tears came from the kitchen and Katie sighed, "That's one of mine," and hurried off to see who was crying.

"Have the police said anything more about how Brian... uh..." Jimmy stammered, looking around the table for support, but found none.

"Died?" Lara filled in for him. "No, they're supposed to do an autopsy. Sheriff Bodie said that was required in cases like this. Apparently there were...irregularities."

Lara's mother gasped. "Not at the dinner table, Lara," Helen corrected stiffly.

But Paul ignored her. "Cases like this? Irregularities?" Paul questioned, worry etched on his face. "They don't expect foul play, do they?

Sally rolled her eyes. "Worried about what the voters will think?"

"Nooooo." Paul drew out the word and Lara could tell that was exactly what he was worried about. She couldn't really blame him. Having a sister suspected of murder would be hell on a political campaign. She'd certainly not wasted a lot of time mourning her husband, and the thought of Will brought a fresh wave of warmth to her cheeks.

An uproar started at the kids' table in the kitchen, so Sally joined Katie to quiet the noise. Jimmy and Paul never broke pace with their eating, obviously knowing their wives would take care of it.

"Why don't you two go check on the kids once in a while?" Lara directed at Paul and Jimmy.

Each paused with a fork halfway to their mouths, looking at her as if she'd grown a third head.

"Men," Lara muttered, hiding her plate of ham beneath her napkin and pushing away from the table. "Dad, can I borrow your truck? The police returned the Buick, but I'd just as soon not drive it."

"Of course, honey," her father agreed without question, digging his keys out of his pocket and handing them over. "Are you keeping the Buick?"

"Why wouldn't she keep the Buick?" her mother interjected. "It's a perfectly acceptable vehicle."

"It may be acceptable, but I sort of feel like I'm driving a murder weapon. I'm putting a sign up at the carnival that it's for sale."

"You're going to the carnival?" her mother questioned, a look of pure horror on her face. "But, Lara, after everything that has happened, don't you think it would be better if you went home?" Her mother paused, then, to clarify, added, "To get some rest?"

The hopefulness in her mother's expression tugged at Lara and she battled inwardly with the dutiful daughter. "I've rested enough, Mom. Besides, it's the best chance I have to get signatures for my petition."

"Petition?" Paul spoke around a mouthful of green beans. Sally and Katie were coming back into the room and Lara eyed the two women with a mix of envy and sadness. She'd wanted to be them for years, with their perfect marriages and perfect kids. Now...Lara wasn't so sure perfection existed.

"Yes." Lara felt a surge of confidence and pity as she looked down at her family seated around the dining room table. "I'm starting a formal petition to encourage the city council to vote down AmeriMart's building permit."

"What?" The collective voices of her entire family echoed up to Lara.

"And I'm starting it tonight."

Chapter Nine

W ill inhaled the sweetness of deep-fried Snickers and cotton candy as it mingled with the deeper aromas of alligator on a stick and fried catfish. The Southern perfumes whirled around the carnival as thickly as the costumed children running from one treat booth to the next. The fall street fair offered an alternative to the traditional neighborhood trick-or-treating, and from the looks of the crowd, it seemed that everyone, regardless of which side of the tracks they were living, had come out for the event.

Will examined faces as he weaved through the crowd, though he didn't find the one he was looking for. He hadn't seen Lara since the council meeting but her face hovered in the back of his mind. There was so much he had to say.

His response to seeing her on the doorstep of his house Thursday morning had been something of a surprise. It was as if the last fifteen years hadn't existed and they were back at the lake on his last night in town. Instead of pushing her away, he'd pulled her closer as he'd wanted to then. There was no guarantee they'd have worked out. He knew that, but at least he'd have tried. He wanted what they couldn't have then. He'd anticipated taking things a bit slower, however.

When he'd learned of the AmeriMart project and its destination, he'd been determined to be the one to bring it to Belle Terre. Will hadn't stepped foot in the town since he'd left in the back of a sheriff's van when he was seventeen. He'd promised himself then he would return someday and show them that he'd made something of himself. He didn't know how at the time, but he'd been working for almost fifteen years to make it happen.

Now all of his work was crumbling away. With a phone pressed to each ear for the last several hours, he had his hands full trying to calm nervous investors and the Ameri-Mart Board of Directors. They were taking a chance on LCB Construction but had liked his connection to Belle Terre.

AmeriMart's parent company had been dealing with image issues, having dealt with some very bad publicity over recent construction in small towns. Lara had hit the nail on the head—many small businesses couldn't compete and faltered once AmeriMart was in place. AmeriMart wanted LCB and, in particular, Will, to make this a painless and quiet build.

Of course, Will was still waiting to receive word from Paul Caldwell that his building permit had been granted by the council. There was also one owner still holding out on selling the property rights to AmeriMart. Of the two buildings standing in his way, only one had been available for sale. The understanding he had from the legal team was that the building was owned by a co-op and one owner was proving illusive. Once that was taken care of, they would break ground in less than a week. The construction crew was arriving in two days, and with it, Will acknowledged, its own problems.

"Will!"

The ring of his name over the crowd stopped Will's inner thoughts and he pivoted to see Paul Caldwell headed his way. Paul was working very hard to appear relaxed as he sidestepped the trick-or-treaters, but it only added to the tension knotted across the man's shoulders. Will couldn't help but wonder if other things weighed on Paul's mind.

"Hey, Paul," Will acknowledged as Paul pumped his hand in greeting enthusiastically. "Is there word on the vote?"

"Not yet. Several of the board members asked for time to review the minutes from today's meeting, but I wouldn't worry about it. Things have never moved quickly in Belle Terre."

"No." Will gave a half-hearted smile. "I guess they haven't."

He sucked in a deep breath. "There's more we need to talk about, Will." Paul scrubbed a hand across his jaw, not quite meeting Will's gaze. "I should have said something earlier...but I wanted some place quiet." He gestured to the swirling carnival rides and the rock station booth just a few feet away. "Not that this qualifies, though." Paul took a deep breath, fisting his hands against his waist. He looked at Will earnestly. "When we were kids—"

"Look, Paul..." Will shifted his feet, wanting to ward off the inevitable conversation of their past. Nothing could change what had happened. Even now, he wondered if anyone would believe the truth. "That was a long time ago. Let's just call it water under the bridge."

Paul's shoulders sagged and he exhaled the breath he was holding. "There's not a day that goes by that I don't regret it."

"In truth, it might have been for the best. I always wanted to leave town and I got to do just that."

Some of the tension eased out of Paul's stance and the deep crease across his forehead. "Still, I'm sorry. Okay?"

Paul paused a minute while a few people congratulated him on the town meeting, offering their support for his upcoming election.

The mayor turned back to Will. "Sorry about that. Have to keep the voters happy."

"Are you running for mayor again?"

Paul shook a few more hands. "That's why I wanted to talk about what happened when we were kids. I'm throwing my hat in the ring for state senator."

Ah. Will understood Paul's need to air things out. It wouldn't serve for the past to be discovered by an opponent during the campaign. Paul had been the one to bring the drugs to the park, but Will ended up being the one to take the fall. "I'm serious about it being in the past, Paul. I've no desire to cause you any grief over that."

Paul clapped him on the shoulder. "You're a better friend than I deserve, Will."

Will and Paul shook hands and Will would admit it felt good to get some of that baggage off of his shoulders. Wanting to stay focused on the future rather than the past, Will pressed on. "Can you tell me more about the owner of the bookstore? The one that won't sell."

"Yes." Paul scratched the stubble on his chin. "Why don't we head back toward the city booth? I can show you more on the map there." He turned to his left and started walking so Will fell in step beside him. "The owner is, or was, Mr. Lautner. I was really surprised when he turned down the offer. He'd talked about retirement last year. Lara even started working for him part-time a few years back so he didn't have to be at the store so much. When AmeriMart started buying the properties, I thought he would be the first to jump on it."

Will had seen this before. It was a usual tactic in his line of work. "You said 'was the owner.' Did something change?"

Paul shook a few more hands as they walked. "You understand the land and building are jointly owned, correct?"

Will nodded. "The River Front Co-op. All the owners have to agree on the sale."

"About two years ago, he filed LLC papers and turned over ownership to the LLC but he retained the title of CEO."

"A limited liability corporation?" Will's mind raced over the possibilities. Maybe he was right and The Book Nook owners were trying to get more money, especially now that they were the last business to stand between LCB and the property it needed for construction. "LCB's paperwork lists him as the owner. If he's not the right person to be negotiating for the bookstore, then why hasn't he told us?"

"Good question."

"Do you know the owner of the LLC?"

"Not yet, but I've got legal working on it."

Will and Paul approached the city booth and Will instantly recognized Paul's parents working the tables. Another woman, the spitting image of a younger Helen Caldwell, was talking to a man in hushed, angry whispers. Several people were gathered round, looking at flyers about upcoming events hosted by the Coalition for Order and Decency. Will remembered one of the speakers mentioned the group at the town meeting. He also noted several stacks of campaign flyers and buttons for Paul.

Paul introduced his wife, Sally, who Will recognized as the council secretary. She didn't look any happier now than she had at the meeting. Paul's parents greeted him coolly and Will could sense the distrust in their once-over. He tried not to bristle at their attitude. Their last memories of him, however false, were not good. Paul also introduced his sister and her husband, who stopped fighting long enough to say hello.

Paul spread the map out on the back table and indicated a large section of land marked in blue. "I had these at the council meeting. This is the plot where LCB has options for the store." He pointed to another circled brightly in red. "This is the bookstore." Paul traced the line of buildings on the map to a point about eight inches from the bookstore, where they intersected another line of buildings.

"This is the other co-opted building I told you about, owned by a group called Cypress Covenant."

Will circled a section of land blacked out on the map. "This is the building that's not for sale, correct?" He shifted his finger between the two buildings. "I have to have one of these two buildings demolished to have main street access."

"Yes," Paul agreed. "About the same time AmeriMart started surveying the land, some law firm in New Orleans filed a lawsuit on behalf of the Cypress Covenant to have this one declared a landmark."

Confused, Will asked, "But weren't all the buildings built about the same time?"

"Yes, but the renovations done in the seventies make the second building ineligible for historical status in my opinion. I'm not sure why the lawsuit was filed, but you know the legal system. It grinds on, if not slowly."

"Am I facing anything similar with the River Front Co-op?"

"According to my sources, no one contacted them about historical preservation."

"So the bookstore owner is the only one keeping me from getting the first building and the lawsuit the second."

"And it can't be sold until the lawsuit is decided by the courts."

"And let me guess." Will leaned against the table, one leg crossed over the other. "That's a few years down the road."

"You got it." Paul folded the maps. "Of course, if the lawsuit is withdrawn, then the land becomes available for sale."

Chapter Ten

After Will and Paul parted company, Will ambled through the crowds, grabbing a cold beer from one booth and some fried alligator from another. After inhaling the gator in a few bites, he followed the crowds to the bakery booth and snagged the last piece of pound cake on the table. As he wiped the crumbs from his mouth, he wasn't sure it was better than sex as the sign proclaimed, but it was a close second.

Thinking about sex, of course, brought him back to Lara. The thing was, they'd barely kissed before today and she'd invaded his thoughts over the last fifteen years anyway. He knew they—*he*—should have slowed things down, but damn, that woman could stir him up. Once she kissed him back, hope went out the window. He was already lost and the realization didn't scare him. The only thing that scared him was the knowledge that Lara was running as fast as she could in the opposite direction. He'd have to do something about that. What that was, however, remained a mystery.

As he walked, a few people nodded in his direction, but most left him alone, either not sure of him or not sure which side of the AmeriMart battle they sat on. Years ago, the behavior would have bothered him, but he'd gotten used to the position his job put him in. When you came to town bringing change, people either loved you or hated you. This time was different, however. This time...this time, he wanted their acceptance.

As he rounded the corner by the ticket booth, squeezing through the long line of parents and kids, he spied Lara near the front of the line talking to the adults. She had a clipboard in her hand and a look of sheer determination on her face. Will hung back, sipping his beer.

The line cleared out and Lara concentrated on her clipboard, occasionally blowing a flyaway lock of hair out of her face. She still chewed her bottom lip when her thoughts were working overtime and Will could only wonder what occupied her mind at the moment. He knew what occupied his, and it centered on her naked.

The indecency of his thoughts must have sent shock waves through the air, because Lara looked up from her scribbling and caught him staring. He took a step in her direction, but she turned and headed deeper into the crowd. Will tossed his beer into a nearby receptacle and had to jog just to catch up with her.

"I thought women were the ones that always wanted to talk. It's supposed to be the guy running in the opposite direction."

Lara leaned her head back and feigned laughter. "Does that mean next time I get to fall asleep right after the mind-blowing sex?"

"So there's going to be a next time?"

"That's not what I meant—"

He took her by the hand and pulled her from the crowds and into a secluded spot behind the cotton candy booth.

When he turned to face her, she was carefully setting her clipboard and pen down on a stack of boxes. Then she leaned forward and pressed her lips to his. Lara held her breath; he could feel the vibration of the pent-up energy hum beneath the surface of her skin. Her kiss was hesitant, seeking permission, approval. So he gave it to her.

With his left hand at the nape of her neck and the other cupping one cheek of her backside, he pulled her into his body and crushed his lips to hers. He was brutal, he knew, as their lips melded together and their bodies tangled. Her arms came up around his shoulders and she lifted her body against his, pressing the hardened length of his cock against her stomach.

Lara lifted one leg around his waist and cocooned him in her warmth between her thighs and Will nearly exploded in his jeans like a teenager. He raised his right hand to cup her breast, feeling the pebbled nub beneath the cotton. Will rolled the nipple between his fingers, feeling her moan against his mouth, and he wanted desperately to shed her of her clothes and have his way with her. She tasted him and teased him with her talented tongue and he could think of little more than her body and his.

With a ragged growl, he pulled away and the scents of flowers and spun sugar and spiced apples filled his senses but didn't overwhelm the freshness that was Lara. "It was mind-blowing, huh?" he rasped, still hard and on the edge. He moved against her again. "Good to know I'm not out of practice."

"Will…" Her voice was breathy and hoarse.

"Lara."

"I shouldn't have done that."

"I didn't mind."

"This is a bad idea."

"I've had worse."

She pushed the hair back from her face and let out an exasperated sigh. He could barely contain the impulse to push aside her clothes completely and touch her everywhere. In fact, it was all Will could do to keep from dragging her into the haunted house and adding a few more moans to the chorus already emanating from the structure across the walkway.

He stepped back, smoothing her skirt, straightening her sweater.

"Walk with me, Lara?" Will asked, backing farther away reluctantly, arms spread wide, palms up. "I'm fully dressed and wide awake."

She lowered her head and gave him a grim look from beneath the dark curve of her eyelashes. "If I hear a single snore..." She pointed a finger at him in warning, but a smile quirked at the corner of her mouth.

Will gestured toward the walkway with his left hand, placing his right hand at the small of her back. "You can smack me like you should have yesterday." He let his hand linger a moment, lost for a second in the intimacy of the touch.

They fell in step together, silent as Will's thoughts scrambled for the right thing to say. He didn't want to scare her off, but he didn't want her to get away, either. He nodded to the clipboard clutched protectively to her side. "Is that petition to convince the council to deny the building permit?"

Lara held it out in front of her and he could see the top sheet was only half filled with signatures.

"Yes. I think the store is wrong for Belle Terre." She paused and greeted two passersby by name, showing them her petition. One signed, the other declined. Ever the beacon of good manners, Lara thanked them both and wished them a good evening. "They built an AmeriMart over in Donnelley two years ago and you wouldn't recognize the place today."

Will let that sink in, remembering the small town just twenty miles southwest of Belle Terre. There was a particularly nice stretch of open land near the river in Donnelley, where he and Lara had been headed his last night in town. As much as he hated to think of Belle Terre changing, he knew that time didn't stand still. Without change, life stopped.

Leaving town as a kid, even in the custody of the state, had been the best change he could have hoped for. It led him to the Marines, then college. Now he was on the verge of a success he'd never dared dream about as a kid.

"Are we talking strip bars and casinos?"

"No," she admitted reluctantly. "Fast food places, mostly. A few businesses closed up. A bookstore, to name one."

"Speaking of bookstores, do you know a Mr. Lautner? Owns a place called—"

"The Book Nook." Lara was suddenly studying her clipboard very intently. "Yeah, I know him. Why?"

A rising murmur drew their attention and a crowd of people tightened ranks ahead of them. Will stretched to see over the crowd but couldn't make out much. The familiar sounds of knuckles meeting skin and bone leaked through the noise.

"I just need to talk to him." He grabbed Lara's hand and pulled her along as pushed his way forward. Just as he broke through the last line of people, he watched a young kid go sailing past him to slide a few feet on the pavement. From the edge of the circle, a young girl clutching a stuffed penguin stepped in front of the boy on the ground as he struggled to rise.

"You stop this minute, Mike," she yelled over the bells and whistles of the carnival, the penguin held out like a barrier. She looked quickly over her shoulder as the boy on the ground managed to get to his knees. "He didn't mean nothin' by it."

"The dipshit attacked me, Bex," Mike replied, leaning forward only to be met by a swift left jab with Bex's penguin. The momentary distraction gave the object of Mike's attention time to push up from his knees and lunge, but Will stepped between the two boys just in time.

"Whoa there, cowboy." He pressed his hand to the kid's chest, recognizing him now from the council meeting earlier today. His nephew. As Mike moved into his line of vision, Will signaled for him to stay back as well with a look.

The smaller kid swiped the back of his hand across his bloody nose and grimaced. His eyes darkened and narrowed in on Mike. "Keep your hands off my sister, asswipe."

Bex turned the penguin in her brother's direction. "Stay out of this, *Vincent*. It's none of your business."

"It is, too, *BeckyLynn*, when this wanksta's telling everyone at school you're an easy lay."

Even in the dim light of the carnival, Will saw the blush creep up the girl's neck and fill her cheeks until she matched the red off-the-shoulder blouse barely clinging to her slight frame. "You bastard! We never!" She pummeled Mike with the penguin as she yelled. "You couldn't get it up but you're telling everyone how easy I am?"

Mike held his hands out in defense, but the crowd started to roar with laughter and his embarrassment quickly turned to fury. Will recognized the violence as soon as it slid like a shadow across Mike's face. The boy raised his fist, growling out the word, "bitch." Will grabbed his wrist in midair. The crowd's laughter died and Will's world narrowed.

"Think again, son." Will's voice fell an octave and he forced himself to remember this was a kid, not his old man.

He saw Lara emerge from the crowd with a hand full of napkins, stopping short as her gaze flicked between him and the kid. Will breathed out the tension tightening his shoulders.

Mike snatched his hand out of Will's grasp and turned to Bex. "I'm done slummin'," he spat out as he brushed past her. She pin-wheeled to keep her balance, her ankles wobbling in the spikey heels strapped to her feet.

BeckyLynn drew back her arm and fast-pitched the penguin at Mike, beaming him in the back of the head. "Limp dick!"

Will swallowed the laugh choking in his chest and went to see how Vincent was fairing under Lara's care. She had his head tilted back and a wad of napkins pressed to his bleeding nose. More blood oozed down his left arm from the road rash where he'd slid into the pavement.

"You going to survive, Vincent?" Will asked, surveying the damage to the kid's arm.

"Name's Steele," Vincent replied nasally, wrenching away from Lara's attentions.

BeckyLynn harrumphed her disbelief. "Don't be such a douche, Vincent," she chided, but there wasn't much derision in her voice.

"I had things covered," Vincent said less-than-convincingly. "Didn't need no help from you."

"Whatever." BeckyLynn rolled her eyes, one hand planted on her hip. "Mike was gonna stomp on your nut sack and grind your little—"

"OK!" Lara interrupted, but Will could also see the laughter twinkling in her eyes. "We get the picture."

Will coughed and cleared his throat. "Uhh...Steele. Didn't I see you at the council meeting today?"

Vincent/Steele looked at Will warily, shrugging his shoulders. "Yeah."

"Are you two Chloe's kids?"

BeckyLynn and Vincent moved closer to one another, eyeing Will like he was a pervert about to pounce. It was good to know that even if they fought, they would back each other up when pushed came to shove.

"What's it to you?" BeckyLynn shouldered her purse, freeing her hands, ready for a fight. The action showed familiarity and Will flinched inwardly.

"Because I'm your uncle."

Chapter Eleven

Will watched his niece and nephew drive off, the one working taillight like a distress beacon in the rising cloud of exhaust pluming behind the ancient LeBaron. Guilt poked at his insides, sharp and insistent. When he'd left fifteen years ago, he'd only thought of what he'd be gaining. Not what he'd be missing. Maybe Chloe was right and he couldn't save them.

Lara cleared her throat and it brought his attention back to her. "I'm going to go."

"I'll walk you back." He slipped his thumbs inside the front pockets of his jeans and turned back toward the fair. A blast of air from one of the cooling fans swirled the hem of Lara's dress around her ankles, and for a second he was yanked back to that last night in town, Lara's cheerleader skirt hiked high on her thighs as they raced down the road to Donnelley on his bike.

Even now, he could feel the weight of her hands in the pockets of his jacket as she clung to him when the bike leaned into a curve. All he'd thought about that night was being with her and finding a way for them to be together. She'd been as trapped by her family as he was by his.

She matched his slow, even pace. "I know that face. That's Will's 'I need to save everyone' face."

"I never saved anyone, Lara." The admission tasted sour and burned his chest when he swallowed.

"Did anyone ask you to save them?" She studied him from the corner of her eye, face void of judgment.

In truth, no one had ever asked anything of Will. He'd always known their expectations, though, and they weren't favorable. For a seventeen-year-old kid, that led to one of two things, unprecedented rebellion or a Messiah complex.

Maybe that was why he'd taken the blame for Paul that last night in town when the sheriff had discovered the bag of weed on the ground between them. Paul was his best friend and had his own set of expectations to live up to. No reason both of them should get screwed.

"No, I guess not," he mumbled, and he wondered for the first time if the expectations he'd failed to live up to were his own, rather than someone else's.

The carnival started to wind down, some of the game booths beginning to close up. The exhibit of the fall flower show winners still looked open and Will could swear he heard Lara growl under her breath as they passed by.

Families walked slowly to their cars. Dads carried sleeping toddlers on their shoulder while moms wrangled with older children hyped up on sugar and adrenaline. He'd always considered his life complete until now. Had things gone differently that fateful night, would he and Lara be heading back to their house with the two-point-two kids and family dog?

"I left town and never looked back."

"I know it's going to be hard to accept, but everyone you

left behind"—Lara made quote marks in the air—"was an adult fully capable of making their own decisions."

"I never said they weren't. It's just that it was…"

Will paused and Lara filled the rest. "Your responsibility?"

Lara knew all about responsibility. She'd been trying to live up to it her entire life, always feeling like she fell short, especially since her marriage had gone south a few years ago. Would Brian have cheated if she'd been able to get pregnant? Not even the doctors had a reason she'd never conceived.

"Yeah, I'm in touch with that emotion," she continued, ignoring the other thoughts jumbled in her brain. She decided to change the subject, retreat being the easier part of denial and all. "Is responsibility why you asked to be the foreman for this job? Here? So you could check up on everyone?"

Will contemplated her question silently, but she couldn't read the expression on his face. She gathered a few more signatures on her petition. She also tried to rein in the giddiness in the pit of her belly at his nearness. That giddiness was what got her naked on the Berber carpet, she reminded herself.

He finally shrugged. "A little, I guess."

There was more he wasn't telling her; Lara would bet on it. But then again, she had her own secrets.

"You'd never met your niece and nephew before tonight, had you?" Lara thought of the slew of nieces and nephews that filled the houses at holidays and birthdays and so many weekends in between. As much as she struggled with her place in the family, she couldn't imagine life without all of them.

"I didn't know about them until after my dad died ten years ago," Will explained. "Once I started working regularly, I tried to send money when I could, but Chloe never responded to my letters. Soon I just stopped writing and kept sending the checks. Maybe it was easier for her to accept the money that way."

Her attention intent on Will, Lara didn't see the group of kids running directly at them until it was too late. One of the bigger kids knocked into her shoulder and she stumbled back until Will's two hands encircled her waist, pulling her against him. Their faces hovered close enough she could see the tiny lines at the corner of his eyes and mouth, the faint scar beneath his lower lip. His pupils retracted to twin pinpricks of darkness in the coffee-colored irises.

"Come back to the house with me," he whispered hoarsely.

Her mind and body filled with memories from their morning together and instead of sending her running from his touch, she leaned in closer. His knee pressed between her thighs and his hands slid up the bare expanse of her upper arm, igniting her own ignored passions. Her skin warmed. Her pulse beat in her throat and places lower.

It wasn't until he moved to kiss her and her mind screamed, *People are watching and will tell your mother!* that she took a step back.

Lara whirled away from Will, the space around her suddenly emptier than ever before. She fought to find words as she took a few halting steps. "I can't do this..."

"Lara, please—"

"No!" She held out her hands to stop him, knowing that if she ended up in his arms again, she'd give in to the emotions pulling at her. She'd end up right back where she was with Brian. "You represent everything I'm trying to get away from."

"I don't understand."

"AmeriMart. Family obligation. I can't...won't...I need to go." Then Lara fled like the chicken-hearted coward and good little girl that she was always expected to be.

Lara hurried through the dwindling crowd back to the city booth where her family was working to support Paul's campaign for state senator and his role as mayor of Belle Terre. Helen Caldwell always volunteered the family to help out with his campaign. Helen called it community service and civic responsibility. Lara called it forced servitude.

To explain her actions for the day, Lara's thoughts ping-ponged between an insanity defense and an alien abduction defense. She'd lost her mind, that was all there was to it, she reasoned. What else could account for the fact that she'd had sex—*mind-blowing sex*, her brain amended—with Will Kenner in the living room of the Hastings's house, but that she'd kissed him in the middle of the Halloween carnival?

Will could always push beyond the carefully constructed walls Lara lived within, walls which kept her in the confines of the family's control, she realized now. Did Will breach them so easily because she was weak, or because she wanted someone to not be scared off and work to get through to her? Brian had never worked for her attention or affection. He'd gained the first because her mother liked him so, and after that, Lara had just accepted him as the next step in her life.

Will had never worked to gain her parent's approval, not that he could have. Helen had been very vocal about her thoughts on the Kenner family, especially after Paul befriended Will. Lara wanted to believe her mother was being protective, but Lara suspected that it had more to do with avoiding gossip.

As she neared the booth, she could feel her mother's disapproval before she turned the corner of the WKRZ booth still blaring classic rock from its speakers. And sure enough, Helen's Superman gaze locked on Lara as soon as she rounded the corner. Lips tightly pursed, hands punched into her hips, Lara's mother radiated displeasure.

"Where have you been?" Her mother's voice, sharp and insistent, poked at Lara's weakened composure.

Lara took a cleansing breath, reminding her that this was her mother. Mothers worried. Mothers stayed awake nights thinking of things to worry about. "I've been getting signatures for my petition."

Helen's long silence and all-seeing gaze told Lara that her mother knew that wasn't all she'd been getting that day, but Lara kept her face blank and her breath shallow, like an opossum playing dead while the bobcat circled.

"I guess that Will Kenner was helping you." Helen's voice shuddered on Will's name. A mother also knew trouble when she saw it. Lara would like to assure her mother that Will wasn't trouble, but he was. Lara just wasn't sure what kind of trouble he represented and whether or not she wanted more of it just yet.

Katie's ears perked up. "Will Kenner? Didn't you two have some sort of steamy, forbidden thing going on in high school?"

"Of course not," Lara said nonchalantly, moving to help pick up a pile of political buttons with her brother's face showing a toothy smile and his disembodied hands giving a two-thumbs-up gesture. "He was Paul's best friend."

Paul turned around in his chair and eyed Lara. "You're hanging out with Will?"

"And apparently he's helping her get signatures for her petition," Katie added helpfully.

Lara continued to a box of fliers, feeling the weight of her brother and sister's stares boring into her back. "He wants them to build the store. Why would he help me get signatures in opposition to it?"

"I'm sure he has his reasons," her mother rationalized, going back to packing up the flyers and brochures laid out on the tables. "I don't know why you have to make such a fuss over this store, Lara."

You mean you don't know why I have to have an opinion that differs from yours, Lara thought. She picked up the stacks of flyers and boxed them. "I don't want to see what something like AmeriMart will do to this town."

"But think of your brother." Her mother pointed to Paul in case Lara had forgotten what her brother looked like. "He's the mayor. What will people say if his own sister doesn't support him?"

"Hey, Paul." Lara turned to her brother, who sat at the back table while his mother picked up his booth. Sally sat at the other end of the table and angled away from him, like they weren't speaking to one another. They'd been quarreling all day and it didn't appear anything had changed. "Do you think I'm not supportive of you as mayor because I oppose the AmeriMart?"

"Course not." He smiled somewhat wickedly. "I didn't vote for you for homecoming queen. Guess now we're even."

Turning back to her mother, she couldn't contain the grin widening across her face. "See? Family's still intact."

Helen didn't respond, which Lara should have known was a bad sign.

Chapter Twelve

S aturday started early for Lara. The doorbell buzzed shortly after seven, waking her from a restless sleep filled with dreams she'd just as soon forget. She grabbed a robe and stumbled to the door. If someone was waking her up to complain about her not mowing the grass this morning, they weren't going to be happy with her response. Lara opened the door, blinded momentarily by the sun haloing off her sister-in-law's blonde hair.

"Hey, Lara," Sally chirped, handing her a large cup of carry-out coffee. "I left Paul."

The tempting smell of caffeine and radiating warmth stunned Lara into comatose silence. Sally's youngest held her hand and started to whine. Lara realized the other three kids were standing behind their mother, along with suitcases at their feet, an odd-looking dog on a leash and a hamster rustling beneath the pine shavings of its cage as if to bury his head so it couldn't see what was coming.

Hefting the youngest onto her hip in a single, fluid movement, Sally blurted out, "Can we move in with you for a bit?"

Not finding her voice, and worried what she would say if she opened her mouth, Lara simply stepped aside and let her brother's family troop into the foyer, suitcases, dog, and hamster in tow. The house had five bedrooms, more than she and Brian had ever needed, thanks to her uncooperative uterus. After all, Sally and the kids were family, so what harm could it serve?

Don't answer that, Lara corrected mentally, thinking back to the last few days of her life. The steam from the cup sashayed a path up to her nose and seduced her with its tempting goodness so Lara sipped the strong brew and let it work its magic on her brain.

While Sally directed the kids in unloading the Suburban, Lara belted her bathrobe and settled in one of the porch rockers with her coffee. She didn't have to be at The Book Nook for a few hours and couldn't remember the last time she'd enjoyed a cup of coffee out on the porch.

The only thing ruining her perfect morning loomed in the driveway, its steel-belted Michelins winking at her conspiratorially. Over the edge of her coffee cup, Lara glared at the car, her brain churning out scenarios where the car ended up a four-foot square of crunched metal.

Try as she might, though, she couldn't keep her attention from drifting to the Hastings' old place, wondering if Will still slept or already prowled the streets, waiting on the decision from the city council. Sadly, she knew the council would pass the measure and she tried to mentally resign herself to the idea of losing her bookstore. Belle Terre was teetering on the brink of economic oblivion and even if AmeriMart was a bad idea, it was the only idea anyone had at the moment.

Sometime during the night, in the hours of restlessness between when she'd gone to bed and risen, Lara had decided that nothing could come of her lustful feelings for Will. It didn't matter that he made her feel more alive in the last two days then she had in the last two years. It didn't matter that his touch set off things inside that convinced her she could take on the world and win.

Being with him just wasn't possible.

Her family would never approve, and whether she believed it or not, they always had her best interest at heart. They would be here when Will left in six months. He'd made it very clear he was only here for the AmeriMart project, and when that was no longer a factor, he would leave her.

Again.

She knew in her heart that he didn't leave her last time. It hadn't been his choice, but he certainly never came back. They'd gone their separate ways before. They would simply do so again.

No, it was better this way, she reasoned dispassionately, and turned her thoughts outward, because looking inward hurt too damn much at the moment.

Across from her house where the houses backed up to the lake, the drapery of moss waved at Lara from the towering Cypress trees peeking over the roofline. Up and down the street, people were already outside starting yard work that wouldn't end for another few weeks. The weather this time of year in Louisiana was as near perfect as it got, still a little warm in the middle of the day, but the early mornings and late evenings were made for porch sitting. A breeze carried the heady scent of fresh-cut grass and the hibiscus from the back garden and drew Lara's attention to her recovering camellia.

"Frick!" she exclaimed, setting her coffee down on the

banister and stepping off the porch. Someone had dug up her camellia during the night. Again!

"Frick!" she semi-cursed again, this time loud enough that her sister-in-law paused on a trip back from the car while juggling a Wii, Playstation, and Xbox with the assorted controllers. The kids dominoed into her from behind, their arms full of toys and other weapons of pint-sized entertainment.

"You really should replant that thing, Lara," Sally observed, nodding at the camellia over the game consoles teetering in her grasp. "Use enough water and the roots might take hold again before the weather turns."

"I'll do that, Sally. Thanks," Lara shouted as she stomped around the corner of the house, flinging open the gate and letting it swing into the fence with a satisfying crash. She made a beeline for the gardening shed at the back of the property, her bare feet squishing into the soft ground beneath her. Thoughts of Candy's blue-ribbon hibiscus last night at the fair burned at the back of her eyes and the less neighborly side of Lara wondered if she'd had anything to do with her camellia's second untimely demise. But Lara couldn't see Candy, with her body by Pillsbury and brains by Fisher Price, going to that much trouble.

Grabbing the shovel hanging on the wall, Lara also spied the chainsaw Brian had bought when the mayor put together a citizen's response team to handle downed trees after a hurricane. Not that Brian had ever used it, but he'd stood around looking like a gay lumberjack in her pink polka-dotted rain slicker. Lara didn't have anything against gay lumberjacks. She just thought Brian did them an injustice holding the chain saw like he knew what he was doing.

With a sense of purpose that felt both strange and wonderful, she took both the shovel and the chainsaw from the shed and returned to the front yard. Lara tossed the shovel next to the downed camellia and narrowed her focus on the uneven boxwood hedge taunting her from the property line dividing her driveway from Candy's. Lara was stalking toward the hedge when Sally and the kids came out of the house.

Sally flung out her hands to the side and clotheslined the kids to a halt. "Wh–wh–what are you doing, Lara?" she asked cautiously as Lara moved toward the Buick.

Lara set down the chainsaw on the driveway and then began to roll up the sleeves of her robe. "Gardening," she responded, pleased the answer to Sally's question sounded so reasonable.

"Gardening? But it's not Thursday," Sally replied, confused. She tried to usher the kids back into the house, but they were having none of it. A show was about to start and they had ring-side seats. "And you're using a chainsaw."

A few of the neighbors began to sidle toward Lara's front yard, apparently getting wind that another spectacle could be unfolding at the Haley household.

"Sometimes you have to cut away what ails you," Lara answered, thinking of more than just the hedge. She bent over to grasp the thing by the handle. A flick of the throttle and choke, a few pushes of the primer button, and Lara yanked the pull chain back with all her strength. Nothing. *Frick*, she thought bitterly. Two pulls later, the thing roared to life. She revved the motor, switched the choke to the off position, and lifted the whirling, grinding monster with both hands.

No wonder men liked these things, she told herself.

Power seeped from the pulsing body of the machine, up her arms and into her body. Lara's entire being vibrated with the control of something so powerful. Maybe she couldn't save Belle Terre or the bookstore. Maybe she couldn't have a torrid affair with the resident bad boy.

But that hedge was toast.

Sally, the kids and the neighbors had formed a little semi-circle around Lara and they took a collective step back as Lara straightened up with the chainsaw clutched in her grasp. When the chain bit into the trunk of the first boxwood, Lara smiled broadly and let out a celebratory laugh.

This is for you, Angelina Williams!

Shreds of bark and leaf shot back at her as the chain chewed through the wood in seconds. Smoke and exhaust billowed from the rapidly dividing trunk and when the first bush fell victim to her rebellion, Lara skillfully guided the chain to the second hedge. It felt good to take control, though Lara knew it was just a bunch of bushes and not anything important.

But she'd sat back and not voiced an opinion, not even when the judge ridiculously ruled the bushes should be divided between the two houses. And over the years, as they'd grown into a monument to stubborn male pride, she'd kept her mouth shut. Because taking a side would have caused friction, either between her and Brian or her and the neighbors. And Lara didn't do friction.

Well the *old* Lara didn't do friction. The new Lara still had some things to work out.

More bushes followed, and in less than three minutes, she downed the entire hedge. As the chainsaw was winding down, she heard the first cry from Candy as she walked stiff-legged across the lawn, hands pressed firmly to her reddening cheeks.

Once the chainsaw screeched to a halt, Lara brushed the

wood chips and leaves off her face and pulled a twig from her hair.

"Send me a bill, Candy," Lara announced, turning on her heels.

She set the chainsaw down long enough to replant the camellia, then replaced the shovel and chainsaw in the shed and went inside to take a shower.

Now for the Buick, she thought triumphantly.

Chapter Thirteen

"Y ou can't be serious," Sally said with a mixture of disbelief and jealousy as Lara ran her hands over the hard, sleek lines of the gorgeous body in front of them. The jealousy may have been in Lara's mind, but that was okay. This was something worth being jealous about.

"I can honestly say I've never been more serious in my entire life," Lara assured her, loving the feel of the leather against her legs and beneath her fingers. She checked out her reflection in the rearview mirror of the Blazing Soul Red Miata and was reminded of her face in the mirror after her carpet mambo with Will. Same look. Damn. No wonder men loved sports cars. It was like good sex wrapped around your body at high speed.

The showroom was well air-conditioned and Lara blamed the cool air for the hardened state of her nipples. She pulled her T-shirt away from her breasts, then closed her eyes, sinking back to let her body mold to the curve of the seat, remembering the way her body had molded to Will's. She wasn't sure which thoughts filled her head more at the moment, sex with Will or the possibility of owning this car. Both had their appeal.

"This is about that man, isn't it?" Sally whispered, leaning over the passenger side door and interrupting Lara's fantasy.

"Uhhh...Mrs. Haley?" said the salesman tentatively.

Lara looked at the pimple-faced salesman, feeling sorry for the kid. "I'll take it."

"Lara!" Sally shrieked and a number of the other customers looked their way.

"Come on, Sally," Lara exclaimed, swinging her legs out of the Miata reluctantly. She'd traded in her sensible shorts for a pair of cut-off jeans and plucked at a loose string on the hem. She pointed to the Buick sitting there so innocently right outside, framed by the massive windows that surrounded the showroom. The aura of disaster hung around it like an albatross. "Who wants to drive around in the death mobile?"

"Uhhh...Mrs. Haley...Actually, we need to talk about..." He gestured to the Buick cautiously as his squeaky voice trailed off. When they drove up, Lara had noticed him checking out the rear of the vehicle with an intense scrutiny. "Your...uh...trade-in?"

Sally came around the hood of the car. "You're only doing this because Will is back in town," she challenged.

Lara pushed to her feet and leaned against the door frame, one leg bent at the knee. She pictured herself in the same position on the cover of Home and Garden with her chainsaw. The mention of Will's name pulled her from her daydream.

She said good-bye to Will last night, she reminded herself, and any future prospects of mind-blowing sex with him. Well, Lara didn't need mind-blowing sex—*yes, you do,* her mind whispered—and she didn't need Will. *But you want him,* her traitorous mind continued.

"I am not," Lara said defensively. "I need a new car."

"Speaking of cars..." the salesman tried once again, his youthful face a little mottled and flushed. Behind him, a few of the other customers gathered and Lara chalked up their nosiness to the awesome car she was about to buy. *Denial...Egyptian rivers,* her mind whispered.

"What's wrong with the Buick?" Sally's challenge had lost some of its intensity and Lara could see her eyeing the interior. The voice activated audio system with more speakers than she could count just begged for some classic rock to blast through the convertible top.

She shrugged. "What's wrong with your marriage? You've had it for fourteen years. It still mostly works, but you're not happy with it, are you?"

Flushing a little, Sally adjusted the scarf at her neck. Lara wanted to rip off the scarf and muss her sister-in-law's perfectly coiffed hair. Even on a Saturday morning, Sally looked ready for a city council meeting.

"I'm sorry, Sally." Lara closed the distance between them and wrapped her arms around her brother's wife. "I know Paul can be dense. He thinks of you like Brian thought me. An employee. Someone to help out in the office or when he needs Christmas cards done." She stepped back a bit and looked Sally in the eye. "I get it."

Sally deflated a bit and the shine of tears brightened her eyes. "Paul just doesn't see me anymore." Dashing away the tears, Sally studied Lara's face. "You light up when you talk about Will. I never saw you like that with Brian. Does Will make you happy?"

Lara thought on that and on all the things she did feel when she was around Will. "I'm not sure how I feel when I'm with Will but that's okay. Will accepts me. All of me." Lara reached up and untied the knotted scarf around Sally's neck, then released the tight knot at the nape of her sister-in-law's neck. She smiled as Sally's loosened hair cascaded around her shoulders, immediately taking five years off her face. "I don't have to worry about keeping up appearances. I can just be me. Does that make sense?"

Sally reached up and finger-combed her hair, dropping her shoulders and letting out a deep rush of breath. "Yeah, that makes perfect sense."

"It doesn't matter, anyway." Lara sighed. "I'm not seeing him again."

"Mrs. Haley!" The salesman's voice shook and he was standing on tiptoe when Lara and Sally turned their attention to him. A look of frightened expectation thinned his mouth into a grim line. Lara waved to the growing semicircle of onlookers, who immediately found something else worthy of attention.

"I don't answer to that name anymore," Lara explained, crossing her arms. "Please call me Lara."

The salesman cleared his throat, adjusting his clip-on tie. "Mrs...Lara. About the Buick."

"Look..." She straightened and read the guy's name tag. "Tyler. My dead husband did a lot of business with your dealership. You know my brother, the mayor? My family does a lot of business with your dealership. We bought the death mobile here. Tell your bosses to buy back the Buick at Blue Book value and I'll take the Miata at sticker price. Everyone wins."

The salesman opened and closed his mouth like a landed fish, but apparently the thought of a sale at sticker value was too tempting to argue with. Spinning on the heel of his loafers, the kid walked back to the offices, leaving Sally and Lara alone with the car and the now-retreating gawkers. Apparently, when no one died, Lara wasn't nearly as interesting.

"You're different," Sally announced, tucking her scarf in her purse. "What gives?"

Thinking of everything that had happened since Wednesday, Lara lifted her hands, palms outward. "I think this is who I always was, Sally. Now there's just nothing standing in my way."

Later that morning, Lara decided to walk over to her parents' house before going into work. She'd changed from her shorts to a skirt she'd had since a college trip to Mexico. The bright colors and flouncy fabric made her feel free and a little wild. Brian always said it was too short, so she'd tucked it in the back of her closet, never to be seen again, but in truth, the hem barely showed her knees. Lara jangled her new car keys against her palm, noting that the kids gave her a wide berth as she entered the living room.

"You gonna do more gardening, Aunt Lara?" asked the oldest, the younger kids looking cautiously out from behind her.

She couldn't help but laugh. "No, honey. I'm done gardening for a while."

Lara had used her dad's copier last night and accidentally left a stack of petitions by the office phone. She wanted to pick them up to bring them into the bookstore, hoping for a few more signatures during business hours. She brushed her hand down the frame of her new Miata as she walked down the driveway. The paperwork sat on her desk upstairs, in her name, Lara Caldwell. It was only the second thing in her name since she'd signed her marriage certificate ten years ago. There was a deep satisfaction in that, she realized.

Keeping to her side of the street, Lara walked with her head down as she passed by the Hastings' place. Even without looking, she knew Will was watching. Things all over her body tingled and the butterflies in her stomach mutated into pterodactyls. He exited through the front door and jogged to catch up with her.

"Hear there was some excitement over at your place this morning," he teased against her ear, and her body warmed out of habit at the low growl of his voice against her skin. He fell in step beside her.

"I don't know what you're talking about." She glared at him playfully from the corner of her eye, then reminded herself of her decision to ignore her lustful thoughts. But he made her feel like a teenager again, all nervous excitement and warmth. "I did some gardening. Big deal."

"The new car. Verrrryyy sexy." The way he drew out the two words hummed along her nerves, which did more tingling she tried to ignore.

"Everyone needs transportation," she replied before she could stop herself. Will really was a bad influence on her. She couldn't even stick to her guns and not talk to the man. Then again, they hadn't done a lot of talking when she went over to his place that first time and that worked out okay.

"And you're having company?"

His hand brushed hers and spirals of yearning wended up her flesh. Lara crossed her arms. "My sister-in-law and her kids are staying for a bit."

"Makes for a very crowded house, I would think," Will

observed. "My house, on the other hand...completely empty."

Lara gave up on her self-declaration to ignore Will. He really was impossible to ignore. Plus, she didn't really want to ignore him. Did she want what he had to offer? She didn't know.

"You should think about getting some furniture, then. To fill up all that emptiness."

He put his hand just above the swell of her backside and guided her with gentle pressure around a cluster of bicycles lying on the sidewalk. As they returned to the concrete, he let his hand drop and Lara missed the touch.

"Anything particular in mind?"

Lara's face heated in spite of herself. "Just, you know, furniture."

"I think we did pretty well without furniture, and there's new carpet in the entire house. I know how you liked the carpet. You should come by and see it."

"No thanks." But she couldn't help laughing.

Lara turned onto her parents' walkway and Will followed. "Hmmm, the parents' house. Isn't it a little soon to tell your parents about me?"

She tried the front door, only to find it locked. Lara bent over to retrieve the extra key from the little birdhouse sitting next to the rocker. "No one's telling *anybody* about *anything*," she said when she stood straight again. She pointed at him with the house key's pistol key ring, then thought better of the threat given the events of the last few days. "There will be no more adventures on the Berber carpet or any other room of your house. You're leaving. I'm staying. It's time to act like grownups and accept reality."

Will leaned against the door frame, blocking her access to the door. "I thought we were acting like grownups in the living room of my house. And at the fair. As for reality...it's overrated."

If she'd been paying attention to such things, she would admit the wicked grin he gave her worked like a charm. She was all tingly and her heart seemed to have fallen much lower in her body. "That. Will. Not. Happen. Again." She punctuated each word with a jab of the key, then pushed him aside to open the door.

She laid her purse and the keys on the small table by the stairs as Will followed her into the house. "I don't think this place has changed since I was here last," he noted, examining the living room and dining room off the main entry.

"Haven't you heard?" Lara hollered over her shoulder as she ascended the steps to the second story, happy and disappointed that he had moved on from trying to seduce her. "Change isn't allowed in Belle Terre."

She was standing at the edge of her father's desk when Will caught up with her, and before she turned around he was nuzzling her neck.

"Certainly some things are allowed to change." The vibration of his voice against her neck brought a cascade of goosebumps across her flesh.

Lara wanted Will like she had wanted him back in high school. Wanted to feel the weight of his touch. Wanted to sink into the comfort, the security of his presence. It wasn't the same kind of security you got from someone you knew would take care of you like she had with her parents or should have had with her ex-husband. *If* she played their games. With Will, you didn't have to pretend anymore. You could just be yourself and not worry that wouldn't be good enough. Will would take care of her, and he wouldn't fail her like she had failed him.

"You're leaving," she said aloud, mostly to remind herself

that this...this...feeling wouldn't last. There would be consequences. People to face. Heartbreak.

"I'm not gone yet," he whispered against her jawline, kissing her lightly.

But she was, and she turned in his arms to kiss him back.

Chapter Fourteen

Will narrowed the distance between them until each breath Lara took put her breasts in contact with his chest. Her nipples hardened. His body did the same. Her breathing quickened. His slowed. Her lips parted. He leaned in.

"You don't want to do this." Lara sounded breathless and unconvinced, but Will stopped anyway, letting his mouth hover near hers. Their breaths mingled, eyes locked. Heat radiated off their bodies and skimmed along the edge of nerves raw with want and need.

"I don't?" Will circled his hands around her waist, amazed at how easily she fit into his grasp. How easily she fit into his life. He pinned her against the desk with his body and a slight moan escaped her throat as his hardness pressed into her softness. "My body disagrees with you." He slipped his hand under Lara's shirt and caressed the hardened nipple beneath the fabric of her bra with his thumb. "*Your* body disagrees with you."

"We're in my *parents'* house. We're in my *father's* study." She tried to take a step away.

He tightened his hold around her waist and pulled her back toward him, not liking the emptiness when she moved away. He needed to be closer. Much closer. Like, inside of her. Yes, he needed to be inside of her. "You didn't seem to mind when you were eighteen."

Her eyes clouded with passion and doubt. "I'm not eighteen anymore."

Will slid his other hand beneath her shirt and found the clasp of her bra. The fabric parted with a simple twist of his fingers. Her mouth formed a small 'o' and her back stiffened. Will held the ends of the bra together with his thumb and forefinger.

"I'm glad you're not eighteen." He rubbed the center of her back with the tips of his fingers, massaging away the tension knotted in her muscles. Slowly, he released the fabric and moved his hands forward, pushing aside the protective barrier of her bra. "When you were eighteen, I couldn't have you."

A shudder trembled along Lara's body. "My breasts are too small."

Will covered the sensual flesh with his palms. "They're perfect." He rolled the erect nipple gently between his thumb and forefinger and Lara's eyes fluttered closed. She let out a soft cry but leaned closer, holding his shoulders for balance. His body tightened as her hips pressed against his erection.

"And I don't have those cheerleader legs anymore."

Will pushed her gently back until her bottom rested on her father's desk, then he parted her thighs with his knee, stepping into the vee of her legs. Her skirt rose to an indecently delicious height.

"You have legs to die for." Lara's mouth crinkled slightly at the corners.

He abandoned one breast and grasped her beneath the knee, raising her leg until she curled it around his waist. Will followed the curve of her thigh to the juncture of her legs. With the tip of his index finger, he touched the silky barrier over her sex. The panties were moist. He made tiny circles against the material, his touch as light as the kisses he breathed upon her lips. A second cry erupted, this time not so soft.

"I'm not any good at this."

He touched the bow of her lip with his tongue, his senses spiraling with the taste and feel and smell of her. "The hell you aren't."

"You fell asleep last time."

Will had the decency to grin sheepishly. "*After*, not *during*. That's an important distinction. And I don't plan on falling asleep this time."

"Are you sure? I mean if you're tired, we could probably—"

Will covered her mouth with his at the same time he slipped his finger beneath the band of her panties and into the wetness of her body. Lara arched against his touch and he felt her sharp intake of breath when his thumb began to move in slow circles against her.

She was hot and tight and her body quivered around his fingers, and the need to satisfy this woman crashed over Will like a tidal wave. He didn't think of his own needs and desires. He didn't think of his own aching body. He wanted only to give Lara pleasure.

He deepened the kiss, teasing her tongue with his, tugging gently on her lips with his teeth. Lara gasped each time Will changed the motion of his fingers or thumb and her body grew wetter with each slow circle.

Will could feel the orgasm grow within her. Her hips

began to move and her body clutched tightly around his fingers. He watched the heat of her arousal mushroom and pinken the hollow of her neck, wash slowly up her throat and explode on her cheeks until she gasped her release and shuddered around him again and again. She kept her eyes closed, the half-moon of her lashes fanning the slope of her cheek just above the light dotting of freckles she no longer tried to hide with makeup.

Damn, her freckles were sexy.

He devoured her mouth once more, then broke from the kiss. With a final swipe of his tongue, he whispered hoarsely, "Don't go away."

Lara's eyes blinked open and she followed his movements. Her breathing quickened as she watched him position her ankles over his shoulders. At his silent urging, she lifted her hips while he did away with her panties. Will caressed the whisper of a garment over her legs.

Silk panties.

He grinned. She blushed.

Red silk panties.

His grin broadened. Her blush deepened.

Red, silk *thong* panties.

"What other secrets are you hiding beneath your June Cleaver exterior?"

Lara pulled the panties from his fingers and tossed the slip of material over her shoulder. "The bra matches."

When he leaned in and let his tongue lap gently against her body, Lara's head lolled back and her heels dug into Will's back. The breath left her lungs in a single rush of air.

Will glided his tongue over her hot skin, making an agonizingly slow circuit from the tiny nub now swollen with passion to the slick sheath clutching against his finger. He removed his finger, heard her sigh disappointingly at the emptiness, then gasp loudly as he slid two fingers back into the moist channel.

He teased her until her moans escalated to the brink of release, then changed his target to the sensitive inner slope of her thigh. The muscles in her legs quivered each time he kissed her, each time he drew his tongue along the curve of flesh, stopping just short of ground zero.

"Please, Will...I need..." Lara entwined her fingers in his hair.

He feathered kisses along her legs, but once again stopped. "Tell me what you need, Lara." Will teased the crease of her thigh and torso with his tongue. Her muscles tensed and low moans rumbled with each raspy breath. She hesitated and Will wanted her to give in on her own. He flicked his tongue once over her clit.

"Oh, I need more of that, Will." The words rushed out on the tail-end of a tortured moan. "*Please.*"

Will captured her body between his teeth and tongue and her throaty moan urged him on. He flicked his tongue against her flesh, suckling gently as he made love to her with his mouth. Lara gasped and groaned and finally cried out. The heat of her release surrounded him, earthy and sweet, like her. Will felt her body quiver as he slipped his fingers from her body. He eased her legs from his shoulders, letting his hands move along the limbs as he moved back into the vee of her body.

Her eyes were closed when he stood. Lara rested on her elbows, her face flushed, her breathing not quite back to normal. When she opened her eyes, Will saw passion mixed with mischief in the sex-glazed depths. She pushed herself into a sitting position and reached for him, catching the waistband of his jeans and pulling him closer. Lara unsnapped the buttons on the fly and slipped her hand inside his jeans.

Her eyes widened and he grimaced. He knew he shouldn't have put off doing laundry another day.

"Somebody's not wearing boxers anymore."

She slipped her hand beneath his bare flesh to cup him and it was Will's turn to shudder. He braced his hands on each side of her hips.

"They get in the way."

She smiled some more and blushed some more and Will held himself still while she touched him, even though he wanted to pin her to the desk and do more wicked things to her body.

"Tell me what you need, Will." Her voice, throaty with desire, skimmed along his flesh. His body swelled even more as her fingers closed around his thickness.

"You."

"Condom?"

"Back pocket."

Lara found the condom while Will pushed his jeans past his hips. Her hands trembled over the cellophane, awkward, uncertain. The valley between her brows furrowed.

"Lara?"

She didn't look up. Crimson slashed her cheeks. Realization dawned in Will's mind as she fumbled with the condom, hands shaking with uncertainty, and the empty places in his heart filled with the sight and smell and taste of this woman. Will pressed his lips to her temple and covered her trembling hands with his. Lara turned her head and found his mouth with hers, letting her lips move over his while his fingers guided hers.

His body ached when he settled against her, easing into her heat with a gentleness he didn't know he possessed. Her body resisted at first, then closed around his need. Their bodies joined as their souls had done years before.

Will drew back slowly, felt himself leave her body, heard her soft moan of disappointment followed by the sharp intake of breath when he rocked back into her. Their bodies slid together, her legs entwined around his waist. He moved. She gasped. He slid deeper.

A car door slammed shut.

Lara gasped again, but it wasn't a good sound this time. Her hands splayed across his chest, not quite pushing him away. "Damn. My *parents*."

Will smiled, grabbed her wrists, and pinned them at her sides. "Sounds like it," he agreed, then pushed himself into her again. The good gasp returned.

"They'll find us," she argued, halfhearted and breathless. A grin tugged at the corner of her mouth.

He nodded. "They might." He slid into her again, softer this time but deeper than before. She moaned loudly. "You want to stop?"

"You stop now and I'll run over you with my car."

Will buried his face in the crook of her neck, nipping at her earlobe while his hips thrust forward. Lara met him, thrust for thrust, arching her neck into his kiss and moving her body into his. Their movements quickened, chasing the need within them both until Lara cried out and tightened around him. Will shuddered his own release, feeling Lara entwine her fingers with his as their bodies melted together.

They were still joined, their fingers intertwined as intimately as their bodies, when the office door opened.

"Lara, honey. Is that—"

Will heard Mrs. Caldwell's strangled gasp a split second before she hit the floor with a *thud*. Her father shielded his eyes but reached out and pulled the office door closed.

Lara laughed out loud, then slapped her hand over her mouth before the second giggle erupted. "Do you have this effect on all women?"

Will eased himself from her body but did not let her go. "Only the ones that see me naked."

Chapter Fifteen

S he and Will had dressed hurriedly once she found her panties. Will helped her father carry her mother to the bedroom, luckily still unconscious. Then they sneaked away like the guilty heathens they were at her father's urging. There would be hell to pay eventually, Lara acknowledged, but it had been oh so worth it.

She knew then, as Will walked her home, that she still loved him regardless of what her brain was telling her. Not the idea of him, not because he wasn't Brian or because he could make her feel sexy with a simple look, but because he asked nothing more of her than to be herself, and with Will, she knew exactly who that was.

He stole one last kiss in the safe confines of her garage, and she breathed like the weight of the world was off her shoulders. Could she love him for the time they had together, then let him go? Lara didn't know. The thought of leaving with him teased the outside of her consciousness, not that he'd asked.

She entered the kitchen through the garage door, their hands entwined, until she had to let him go to close the door. Head resting against the doorjamb, she breathed to calm her senses. Inside, Sally busied herself settling the kids, dog, and hamster into the house while Lara once again showered and changed before heading into the bookstore.

Hours later, still grinning at her naughty secret, Lara stood behind the counter at The Book Nook, once again the epitome of decorum. The store was busy, which was good, but Lara suspected most had come to see what kind of breakdown she'd have next, which was bad.

All she'd wanted to do was be herself, to escape the expectations that kept her quiet and docile and oh-so-boring. At least boring until Will's return to town, she reminded herself.

But, okay, she would admit that taking a chainsaw to the hedge this morning may have been a bit of overkill. Not to mention having sex in her father's study. Pleasing others her entire life hadn't made her happy, but it also hadn't had her neighbors or family contemplating a call to the state psychiatric hospital.

She sorted through a recent shipment of new releases, ignoring the whispers and sideways glances while she updated the inventory in the computer program she'd installed a few months back. Her body still quivered with the memory of Will's touch and she had to re-count the stacks of books several times to get it right.

Mr. Lautner shuffled back from the science fiction section and sidled behind the counter with her. His plaid seersucker ivy cap sat slightly eschew on his scalp and the crookedly buttoned cardigan hung down his lanky frame. He'd looked that way every time she'd come into The Book Nook since the eighth grade. His hair was a little whiter and a little thinner, but not by much. He'd already heard of her little gardening episode by the time she'd come into the store at ten.

"If you looked up real sudden and shouted 'boo,' I think a half dozen of these nosy Nellies would wet themselves."

Lara laughed, the lighthearted banter feeling good. She pushed the next stack of books ready for the shelves toward him, running her fingers over the glossy covers. Goodness she loved the feel of a new book. "Let me at least run home and get my chain saw first."

Mr. Lautner gave her a small harrumph and cradled the books into the crook of his arm, leaning against the counter so their heads were side by side. "We have a *borrower* on aisle two."

Lara looked slowly toward the classical section, recognizing Will's niece from last night. She wore a hooded sweatshirt about two sizes too big for her petite frame and a pair a jeans Lara was certain wouldn't come off without surgical intervention. "What is she *borrowing*?"

"Animal Farm," Mr. Lautner responded, keeping his attention on the books in his arm and not their young shoplifter.

"Sophomore English," Lara replied as BeckyLynn casually moved toward the door and slipped out with an incoming batch of customers. "We've sold about a dozen copies today."

"So we're ignoring it?"

"Yes, please."

Mr. Lautner kissed her cheek and Lara swatted away the old man's attention. "You're too good."

"We can afford to ignore a few things now and again."

"Speaking of ignoring..." Mr. Lautner started. "You can't keep ignoring our little problem," he warned in a hushed tone. "You said you'd handle it when the time came, and the time is here."

"I know."

Admitting to owning the bookstore was the least of her problems these days. She knew her family wouldn't understand the need for her to have a business when Brian had always been a decent breadwinner. They wouldn't get her need to have something on her own. They'd also discover her other little secret, and that was something she wanted to avoid a little longer. Forever, if possible. Finally she sighed and whispered, "I'm working on it."

Lara stifled a groan as another wave of lookie-lous clambered out of the shop without buying anything. Sally breezed in just moments later with Paul on her heels. The four kids followed like a gaggle of baby ducks. Judging by the looks on her brother's and sister-in-law's faces, if her customers wanted drama, they were going to get it.

"Sal, you're being ridiculous," Paul whispered between clenched teeth while he smiled like there was nothing wrong. "I told you we could work things out."

"I did work things out." Sally walked to the children's section and rapidly pulled a book from the shelf. She motioned the kids over to the cushioned reading area, instructing the oldest to read to the younger ones. Smart kids that they were, they went without protest. "I moved in with Lara."

"Think about the children." Paul gestured widely to his kids, who'd settled into the plush cushions on the floor, happily ignoring their parents. They didn't seem any worse for the wear to Lara.

"I'm the only one thinking about the kids these days," Sally shot back, hoisting her purse higher on her shoulder. Lara noticed she'd sacrificed her city council look for a pair of nice-fitting jeans and a tailored shirt. "All you think about is your campaign."

Paul cradled his head between his hands. "But that's our future!"

"*Your* future, you mean," Sally said, giving a little finger-wave to two women openly staring at them. "I don't remember being consulted on whether or not you should run for state office."

The other customers were beginning to gawk like children in a candy store, so Lara ushered the two of them into her office and shut the door. Not that it helped. They took their newfound privacy to heart and stopped trying to whisper their argument, and boy, did their voices carry. Through the walls. The air conditioning vents. Even the floor vibrated.

She spied a customer trying to take her picture from behind the new display of Angelina Williams's books. Before she could yell at him to "watch out," he'd knocked over several stacks of books and the display sign for the latest release. Lara rushed over and the clumsy customer beat a hasty retreat out the door.

Frustrated, she dropped to the floor to retrieve the fallen books. The bell over the front door jangled again and Lara looked up, expecting to see more customers, but instead met Will's grinning countenance.

"I've never brought a woman to her knees by just walking in a door," he joked, bending down to help her get the remaining books.

The faded jeans he wore stretched tightly across muscled thighs, but Lara tried to ignore it. She also wanted to ignore the woodsy scent of his aftershave and the way his button-down shirt matched his eyes, but ignoring the jeans was as far as she got.

"No, but you did make my mother pass out cold." She laughed.

"Just think what we could do if she'd come in a few minutes earlier."

"I could like you," Lara mocked, accepting the hand he offered when she went to rise.

Actually, she more than liked him, she admitted once again to herself. Her small hand fit easily into his larger one and the jolt of warmth that leaked from his fingertips to her wrist spread wickedly downward. "Of course, people think I'm crazy right now, so take that for what it's worth."

"Unless I turn into a boxwood hedge, I think I'm fairly safe."

He pulled her to her feet, and the nearness of him stole her breath and a few other things she wasn't sure she needed at the moment. Lara turned away so she would remember to breathe. She re-stacked the books neatly on the table, tracing her finger lightly over the author's name on the cover of the book.

When she looked up, she finally noticed BeckyLynn standing behind Will, her face a grim mask. The thin line of her lips said irritation, but it was terror in her eyes.

"Hi, Bex," Lara greeted but Bex did not respond.

Will held out his hand and she begrudgingly pulled the purloined copy of Animal Farm from her purse and slapped it into his outstretched palm. "She had this. No receipt. It's got your store stamp on the inside cover."

"Yes, Animal Farm. They're reading it in Mrs. Hudson's English class over at the high school." Lara smiled at Becky-Lynn, wondering what it was like for the young girl. Like her, BeckyLynn was saddled with her own set of expectations. "Good book. You should enjoy it a lot, Bex."

"So she bought it?" Will asked in hushed tones.

"Barter system," Lara explained on the fly. "I saw Bex's charcoal sketches at the art fair and was impressed. She's going to do a family sketch with all the kids and grandkids for my parents' anniversary next month."

BeckyLynn's mouth fell open, but she quickly recovered and snapped it shut. "See. Told you I didn't steal it." The teen snatched the book from Will's grasp and rushed from the store.

Will's gaze followed his niece then he turned back to her. "Thanks."

"Don't thank me. You've met my family. I got the better deal in that bargain."

Will laughed and gestured to the crowd. "Business is good."

"Drama makes for good business. I'm sure the grapevine is working overtime this morning."

"It's Saturday." Will picked up one of the books on the display table. "There never was much to do in Belle Terre on a weekend." He turned the book cover toward her. "Is this the infamous Angelina Williams the Coalition for Order and Decency is so opposed to?"

Heat warmed her cheeks. "Yes," she said tightly.

She pulled the book from his fingers and returned it to the table, then began to weave her way through the customers back toward the checkout counter. "Not that any of them have ever read one of the books. They're not por-no-gra-phy." The waggle to her hips came back with the slow pronunciation of the word and Lara suppressed a self-effacing grimace. "They're romance. Empowering women to take charge of what they want and who they want it with. Why would the COD people have a problem with that?"

Will laughed, hands up in mock surrender, at her little

tirade, and Lara smiled apologetically. "Sorry. It's a little personal for me."

"I can see that. I'm guessing they're not your favorite people?"

"It's a mutual dislike. Their fearless leader is my neighbor," Lara explained.

"Owner of the recently deceased boxwood hedge?"

Lara tried to contain the wicked smile that tugged at the corners of her mouth. "One and the same."

He turned a book over in his hand, glancing at the back cover blurb. "Maybe I should buy a copy. You know, for research. Get some tips from Angelina Williams on what women like."

She pulled the book from his grasp and plunked it down on the table. "Trust me. You don't need any pointers."

Chapter Sixteen

Will smiled at the wicked look Lara gave him, resisting the urge to run the pad of his thumb over her mouth or tangle his hands in the loose curls framing Lara's face. What he'd do after that was anyone's guess and judging by the number of people watching their every move, it wouldn't take long for the Belle Terre grapevine to explode with the news.

"As for your neighbor, you know what they say, there's no such thing as bad publicity. I'm sure sales will go up the more loudly the coalition complains."

Lara wiggled behind the man working the cash register and started to bag a customer's purchases, the Angelina Williams book on top. Will cocked his head toward the stack of books and gave her his "I told you so" look.

Once the customer was gone, Will extended his hand to the older man. "Will Kenner."

The man peered at Lara nervously, then accepted the handshake but didn't offer his name, which told Will that he must be Donald Lautner. Lara's anxiety seemed to ratchet up a few notches as well, and Will couldn't help but sense a conspiracy between the two. What they were conspiring about, however, he couldn't guess.

"If you're Mr. Lautner, I was hoping to talk to you about the offer AmeriMart made for this property," Will said. Neither Lara nor Mr. Lautner met his gaze. "I understand from the mayor that the property is owned now by an LLC."

"That's right," Mr. Lautner finally replied. He fidgeted nervously with the cash register while Lara pulled out a stack of receipts and shuffled them around.

Knowing Lara's opposition to the upcoming construction, Will had wanted to speak to the store owner alone, but Lara didn't seem inclined to leave. "Is there a place where we could go and talk?"

Lautner glanced quickly in Lara's direction, then over Will's head at the busy store. Loud, muffled voices were coming from behind a door marked "office."

"Lara's just about to go on break and I can't leave the counter unattended."

"I was hoping you could tell me who's able to negotiate the contract being offered for the property," Will said, reminding himself to be patient when Lautner didn't answer right away. Sometimes people would tell you what you wanted to know if you gave them the time. Donald Lautner appeared content with his silence, however.

"That's sort of hard to say," Mr. Lautner finally offered.

Confused, Will prodded harder. "Why is it hard to say? You're listed as CEO, but not owner, and not even the co-op paperwork lists the owner beyond the LLC. Do you know who owns the store?"

Mr. Lautner continued to stare holes into the cash register. "That's kinda hard to say," he repeated.

Will felt a little bit like he was being played for a fool, not a feeling he relished, but again he sensed there was more going on here than just a business owner trying to finagle a higher price on a deal. His only consolation was that the city legal team was looking into the ownership, so he figured there would be an answer sooner or later.

He withdrew his wallet from the back pocket of his jeans and pulled out a business card. Grabbing a flower-topped pen from the canister by the register, he jotted down his number on the back and slid the card across the counter. "This is my cell phone. Maybe you can pass this on to the owner and have them call me."

Mr. Lautner didn't pick up the card but nodded his head once. Will figured that was the best he was going to get for now. He tipped his head in Mr. Lautner's direction. "Thanks for your time."

Lara's entire body vibrated with nervous energy, her shoulders tight and drawn upward to her ears. Will needed to get to the bottom of The Book Nook mystery.

The construction crew would be arriving tomorrow and his timeline grew short. He still waited for Paul Caldwell's call with the news that the city council had approved the building permit. Of course, they could reject the permit, which introduced a whole new set of complications he didn't want to think of yet. He focused his attention on Lara, who studied the papers in her hand with more intensity than necessary.

Before he could speak, the door to the store office opened and Sally Caldwell whipped past the counter. She collected her children from what looked to be the children's section and rushed out the front door. It wasn't until Will looked back toward Lara that he noticed Paul coming from the office. His face was flushed, and like last night, his tie was pulled loose at an open collar.

Paul straightened up, adjusting his collar before coming

over to Will. "I have good news, Will," Paul announced, looking a little off-balance but recovering quickly. "The council voted to approve the building permit."

Lara gasped and Paul gave her a sharp look.

The tension in Will's neck and back eased somewhat, but a knot of concern tightened in his stomach. He looked to Lara and Mr. Lautner. "Now all I have to do is convince the bookstore owner to sell. If I can find out who the bookstore owner is."

Paul waved away his concern, eyeing his sister oddly. "Not a problem. As I told you last night, I had the city lawyers look into it and the legal department says we are within our rights to take the store by eminent domain."

Lara's jaw fell open and her face paled. "You can't do that. You're only doing this because Sally moved in with me," Lara accused bitterly.

Paul squared his shoulders. "As mayor, I can. The development of this land is key to Belle Terre's revitalization."

Will didn't like the news. He especially didn't like the way Lara looked as Paul stood there looking both defiant and victorious. Something was happening between the two of them that he didn't understand. Will wanted to bring business to Belle Terre, not steal a livelihood. The land and businesses he'd bought had been voluntary. This was something entirely different.

"I don't know, Paul. Voluntary sale of the land is one thing. Eminent domain...I'm not sure I'm comfortable with that."

Paul shifted nervously from foot to foot, a tight, thin-lipped smile creasing his face. "It's already done, Will." He pulled an envelope from his back pocket and handed it to Lara. "Lara Caldwell, as owner of the Book Nook, the town of Belle Terre hereby gives you a notice of eviction."

Chapter Seventeen

Once he'd delivered the *coup de grâce*, Paul made a quick exit. Judging by the look on Lara's face, he'd narrowly escaped a fate much worse than the boxwood hedge.

"Let's go outside," Will said, and Lara nearly jumped out of her skin. She was on edge and he wondered why she'd kept the bookstore ownership a secret. He let the new information rattle around his brain. What did it change? There were still people to which he was accountable. Investors. Crew members. Family.

Why didn't she tell me? he asked himself over and over again.

The color had faded from her face and her hands were shaking as she slid the notice of eviction in the bottom drawer.

"I'll be back in a few minutes, Mr. Lautner." Lara patted the elder man on the shoulder, then shimmied behind him and led the way to the front door.

Stepping onto the sidewalk outside, he let his gaze wander up and down Main Street while Lara took a few deep breaths. In every store window along the street, signs announced "going out of business" or "moving sales." In every window, that was, except The Book Nook. They weren't scheduled for demolition until after Thanksgiving, so Will figured there was time to work on things.

Cars moved in a slow line as drivers searched for a space in the limited parking area. Pedestrians strolled atop the blocks-long sea-wall, a fifteen-foot reinforced wall that protected the city, along with the levees, from flooding during hurricane season. Carved into the wall was the town's name along with graphics of cypress trees heavy with moss, shrimping boats, fishermen along the bank of the bayou and oil rigs from the Gulf. It was a pictorial story of everything that made Belle Terre beautiful and special, from industry to entertainment. But he'd been responsible for taking a part of the town that made it special to Lara, and that nagged at him.

Will guided Lara across the street with his hand at the small of her back, remembering the intimacy of their encounter only hours earlier. It seemed another lifetime, however. Lara and Will joined the line of visitors climbing the stairs to the top of the wall.

"You could have told me," he said as they crested the top, taking in the line of shrimp boats and pleasure boats docked at the marina. Behind them stood the line of stores Ameri-Mart was trying to buy, and above that, Will could see the empty land where the AmeriMart would hopefully stand.

"Would it have changed anything? Would LCB Construction go elsewhere with their project because you and I have a history?"

Their shoulders brushed as they took a seat on a bench overlooking the marina, and Will resisted the urge to put his arm around the back of the bench and pull her closer. The red dress she wore really set off her tanned arms and legs and the wide collar framed the oval curve of her face.

"I'd like to think we have more than just history, Lara. I'd like to think we have a future, too."

She sighed heavily and leaned back against the bench, stretching out her legs and crossing her ankles. "Thanks to LCB, my future just went up in smoke."

Her words scraped across his conscience. He needed to tell her other things, but the timing couldn't be worse. Would he only be pouring salt into her open wound?

"I used to love coming up here as a kid," Will admitted, changing the subject. The choppy waters slapped at the pier and the boats bobbed and listed in motion with the winds and waves. "I worked a couple summers on a shrimp boat. Good money for a kid."

"It's good money for a lot of folks," Lara added, pushing a curl of windblown hair behind her ear. She tucked the flapping hem of her skirt beneath her. "The oil spill, the hurricanes, the economy…it's been tough for Belle Terre."

Will listened to the words between the lines, knowing the economic concerns for a town like this. With the diminishing income from fishing and drilling, people needed jobs. It was one of the things he hoped to deliver with this project. "AmeriMart could provide some stability. Jobs. Stronger customer base. Increased tax revenue."

"I know. And I'm just one person. The good of the many versus the one and all that," she admitted.

"But knowing that doesn't make it easier to lose something you've worked to build."

"No," she said sadly. "How long have you worked for LCB?"

Will hesitated. The truth tripped on his tongue. It would come out sooner or later. It's not like he ever intended on hiding it, but he didn't want to set up yet another barrier between him and Lara. "The company's been in business for about five years. This is their first major contract, though. It's a big deal for the owner."

"I know the feeling."

"Why keep the store a secret? Why go through the LLC rather than just put your name on the deed?"

Lara shook her head, then examined the empty ring finger of her left hand. "There was never anything I could call my own. Nothing that said Lara Caldwell was here." She gestured with her hands to the air around her. "I needed that. Otherwise, I'm nothing more than what other people made me. But to get it, I had to disturb the ebb and flow that made up my family, and things with Brian were pretty bad." She paused, staring out at the water. "I just needed to get away from being what they all expected."

"But you don't have to give up on the dream. Can't you just change it a little? Move to another location?"

She shook her head sadly. "Those downtown buildings have been there since the late 1800s, built right after a fire tore through the originals. The whole town worked on them, giving lumber or labor or whatever they had. Like they were all saying, 'We're still here and we're coming back stronger than ever.' That's what it means to me as well. I've been lost, maybe even overtaken by what other people need and want. This was my way out. Can you understand that?"

"More than you know," he admitted.

"Is that why you didn't tell anyone the truth the night you were arrested at the lake?"

Lara was watching him now and he felt the intensity of her gaze straight through to his backbone. He cleared his throat, tried to make comprehensible in his head what he'd never said aloud.

"You can't come with me." Will tried to reason with her, but his hands still burned where they'd touched her skin. He'd told her he was leaving town and she was willing to throw it all away and go with him. Family. College. For him. His jacket swallowed her small frame and he fisted the collar in his hands. "You can't save me, Lara. Don't even try."

"Why not? Because of my parents? I'm eighteen. I can do what I want."

"You would never hurt your family. And even if you would, I wouldn't let you. Not for me."

"What's going on here?" It was Paul, and he stood so close when Will spun around that Will could smell the faint odor of pot and the stronger odor of alcohol that swam around his friend. The whites of his eyes were a roadmap of fine, red lines.

"You shouldn't have brought her up here, Will." Paul slurred his words but the tension in his body was clear. "You shouldn't be doing anything with her."

"Leave it be, Paul," Lara warned, and when Paul leaned toward her Will put his body between them even more. "This isn't your business."

"You're my sister," Paul spat at her, then jabbed his finger into Will's shoulder. Bitterness and something harsher twisted his face. "And he's supposed to be my best friend. Friends do not bring sisters out to the lake."

"I am your friend, Paul," Will whispered under his breath, conscious of the gathering circle of people behind his bike. Nothing like a fight to break up the making out. Will reached out to take the keys from Paul's grip. "Let me take you—"

The punch landed awkwardly on Will's jaw and his head snapped to the right. He felt the warmth of blood trickle down his chin where Paul's class ring connected. Lara yelled over his shoulder, but Will threw out his arm to hold her back as Paul launched forward with an attack. Sirens sounded in the distance, but Will was too busy trying to hold Paul off without hurting him. Then it was the sheriff getting between them, grabbing them by the necks and shaking them both to quiet them down.

The crowd melted back into the night and car engines roared to life all around them as people suddenly found something better to do than make out by the lake.

"What's this?" Sheriff Bodie asked, releasing Will for an instance as he bent down and picked up something from the ground. He shined his flashlight and turned the bag of pot over in his hands. He looked first to Will, then to Paul, then back to Will. "Whose is this?"

The weight of his life rushed toward Will. He looked to his best friend, who stood open-mouthed and silent. Lara's eyes ping-ponged between him and her brother. Her mouth opened to speak. Will couldn't hurt her. He'd loved her as long as he'd known her. So he did the only thing he could. He protected her.

"It's mine," Will answered before Lara could say anything and he was sure his heart stopped beating.

"No—" Lara started, moving toward him and the sheriff as he led Will away. Paul remained quiet and let his girlfriend pull him away.

"Let it be, Lara," Will said over his shoulder, a gruffness in his voice.

"I have to do something." Lara sobbed, each tear wearing away another corner of Will's heart.

As Will was put in the back of the sheriff's car, he took one last look, then said simply, "No, you don't."

He took a deep breath, letting go of the memories. "What do you mean?" It wasn't his place to tell Paul's secrets. His sister had guessed when she'd come to the jail to scream some sense into him the morning after his arrest, but in the fifteen years since that night, he'd never confirmed the truth to anyone.

"I'd been wearing your jacket, Will. I knew those drugs weren't yours. They couldn't have been."

Will leaned forward, resting his elbows on his knees. He stared at the darkly moving waters. "Paul had everything in front of him."

"And, what...you had nothing?"

"What I wanted, I couldn't have." He turned his body toward her and crooked his knee onto the bench, laying his arm behind her shoulders. "Paul could. You could. But not me. The town decided what I was long before that night, so living up to their expectations was easy. And it's like you said. It was an escape. I don't know if I realized it at the time, but it was my chance to be something other than Royal Kenner's kid."

"Did Bodie know?"

"He guessed. He had me in the back of the car going to the station and he was giving me his best tough cop voice. He said, 'This is your last chance, boy.'"

"But he let you take the blame for Paul."

Will shrugged. "What else could he do? Besides, it all turned out for the best. I was leaving town anyway. This way, I finished school. Joined the Marines. Got through college working construction and with a GI loan."

"You've done well, then." Lara eased back against the bench and some of the tightness in her shoulders disappeared. "I'm sure your boss will be pleased with your work."

His conscience prodded him. "But I never wanted it to cost you so much. I had no idea about the bookstore. There's a way to work this out."

He said the last part more to himself than Lara, but she remained silent. Will wanted to press the issue with her, but the growing rumble of large engines filled the air. Will and Lara turned to watch several RVs, a flatbed trailer carrying a bulldozer, and two monster SUVs roll down Main Street.

"She always did have impeccable timing," Will grumbled and pushed to his feet.

"She? She who?"

Will wanted to believe it was jealousy that he heard in Lara's voice, but it could have been irritation as well. He didn't answer and Lara followed on his heels as he quickly took the steps down to the street and joined the growing crowd of spectators. Men began pouring out of the RVs and Will went over to shake hands with the crew.

"Where is she?" he asked JJ Webster, the assistant foreman.

JJ plucked the baseball cap from his head and wiped his considerable forehead with the back of his sleeve. Then he pointed to the first SUV. "Where else? In the lead."

Will turned to Lara to tell her to meet him later, but the object of his question was already two steps away, a knowing smirk punctuating her sharp features. Before he could say anything, she was there, holding out her hand to Lara. Mischief glittered in the arctic blue depths of her eyes.

"Riley Kenner. Nice to meet you."

Lara accepted the handshake, the line between her eyebrows narrowing as she gave Riley the once-over. "Kenner? You're related to Will?"

Riley laughed, a deep, throaty laugh that contradicted the petite frame from which it emanated. "Not since I divorced him."

Shock widened Lara's eyes and Will's world slowed to a painful crawl over broken glass. "Why don't we—" he started the same time Lara asked, "And you still work together?"

"I'm the best construction foreman east or west of the Mississippi. He knew better than to fire me after the divorce."

Lara's mouthed the word *foreman* and she turned the full weight of her stare on Will. "But I thought you were the foreman for LCB Construction."

And before Will could answer, Riley filled in the blanks for Lara.

"Foreman? Honey, he *owns* the company."

Chapter Eighteen

L ara pushed her way through the crowd. She knew there would be a price to pay for her rebellion. You didn't go against generations of ancestral Caldwells without paying a price.

All Lara ever wanted was a little happiness, something she could take pride in, and while she adored her family, she wanted her own identity separate from what they'd decided she should be. She wanted someone to love her for herself, not what she could do for them.

Is it too much to ask? she wondered.

Apparently, the answer was yes.

Knowing that the bookstore was the only thing to stand between LCB Construction and the AmeriMart project, Lara wondered if Will had played her for a fool. Had he found out she was the real owner of The Book Nook before Paul's announcement, and his sex-on-the-Berber-carpet routine was nothing more than a ploy to seduce the property away from her? Even though that didn't make sense, she couldn't convince herself otherwise at the moment, and she wasn't going to get much time to ponder the logic of it, because the sheriff and his deputy waited outside The Book Nook when she returned.

"Hey, Bodie." She leaned her head back to meet the gaze of the new deputy more than a foot over her own head. "Jackson," Lara said and she heard the exhaustion in her own voice. "You here to arrest me?"

Sheriff Bodie LaBeauf removed his hat as Lara approached and scratched the dent in his forehead where the rim marked his skin. Jackson just looked uncomfortable but remained quiet.

"Not yet." But he didn't smile when he said it.

"Then what can I do for you?" Lara opened the door to the bookstore and led Bodie and Jackson in, their boots plodding loudly on the wooden floors. Every customer turned, but Lara ignored the gasps and pointing fingers. Even Mr. Lautner appeared a little taken back by the sheriff's appearance.

"It's about Brian, Lara. I have some news." Bodie pointed toward the door marked "private." "Maybe we'd better go to the office."

"Like half the town won't know what you tell me by supper tonight." Lara thought of the female deputy bawling at the crime scene. "How much worse can my life get? Come on, Bodie. What's going on?"

Bodie scrubbed a hand through his graying hair. "Brian died of a heart attack." The words rushed out.

Lara moved behind the counter, ignoring the stares of the customers milling about the store. "I know he was young, but did you see the number of fast food wrappers in the back seat of the car? The man lived on double cheeseburgers and chili fries. And then there's his family history—"

"Actually," Bodie interrupted. "The heart attack was caused by an overdose."

"Overdose?" Lara struggled to comprehend the news. "There has to be a mistake. Brian wouldn't take aspirin. He liked to complain too much about the headache."

Jackson looked so uncomfortable that Lara almost felt sorry for him. Bodie fingered the collar of his tan shirt, pulling like it was too tight. "The initial tox screen didn't show anything unusual, but there were...signs...that something wasn't right."

"Signs?" Lara asked, perplexed by Bodie's reluctance. "Come on Bodie. Spill it."

"At the time of death, Brian was suffering from"—Bodie paused and pinched the bridge of his nose, closing his eyes as the next word exited in a rush—"priapism."

Lara choked on the breath caught in her lungs and the interior of the store swam in her vision. She leaned against the wall behind the cash register. "Wh–what?"

"Please don't make me say it again," Bodie begged.

"But couldn't that just be...you know...rigor mortis?"

"Apparently there are ways to tell what was pre-mortem and what was post-mortem." He retrieved a small notebook from the pocket of his shirt. "According to the coroner, tests show Brian had an unusually high concentration of"—he paused, then read the words slowly—"sil-den-a-fil citrate, ta-da-la-fil and...another drug I can't pronounce in his system."

"And that means exactly what?"

Swallowing first, Bodie blurted out, "Brian OD'd on drugs used to treat erectile dysfunction."

And that was when Lara realized her life really could get worse.

She covered her face with both hands and bent over at

the waist to find some air closer to the floor, because all the oxygen above had been sucked out of the room. The town was going to have a heyday with this information.

"Frick."

Maybe closing the store would be a good thing. She could go into hiding and not have to face anyone. Her thoughts went back to the idea of being a nun. Could you be a nun if you weren't Catholic?

She straightened up, pushed back her hair, and exhaled sharply. "Bodie, the man had five girlfriends. He had his hands full. Both of them."

"I know this is hard—" But at Lara's disbelieving stare and Jackson's choked-back laugh, Bodie quickly sidestepped the innuendo. "*Difficult*. I know this is *difficult*. We'll be interviewing his...girlfriends. See if they know anything about the prescriptions. Can you tell me who was Brian's primary care physician?"

Lara shook her head at the mention of the doctor, thinking back to Candy's comments earlier this morning. "Douglas Barr. He hasn't seen Doug that I know of, but we weren't exactly close the last three years."

"I'm sorry about all this Lara," Bodie offered, shutting his notebook. "The coroner is releasing the body to the funeral home this afternoon. Anything else I can do for you?"

"Yeah," Lara said, thinking about her poor camellia. "The night Brian died, he was trying to dig up the camellia."

Bodie grinned. "Brian never did well with losing, did he?"

"No," Lara answered. "I replanted it, but someone dug it up again last night."

"That's odd. Who else beside you and Brian would care about that camellia?"

"No clue."

Bodie sat his hat back on his head and replaced the notebook in his pocket. "I'll have patrol keep an eye out on your street." He crossed his arms across the wide expanse of his chest, but it just brought more attention to the expanding girth around his middle. "I hear you have some new roommates over at the house."

Lara kept a straight face. She knew how it felt to have everyone swarming like a nest of yellow jackets in your life. If Sally and Paul were splitting up, it was no one's business but theirs. "Sally and the kids are visiting for a bit. To keep me company, you know. In my period of mourning."

Bodie touched the brim of his hat and smiled. "Visiting. I like that. You always were the sweetest thing, Lara. Brian was a fool."

"Thanks, Bodie."

Chapter Nineteen

W ill followed Riley back to the SUV and slid into the front seat while she took her place behind the steering wheel.

"So, did you win her over yet?" Riley asked as she started the engine.

Will had the good sense to ignore the question. "You're a day early. Anything wrong, or did you just make good time from the job in Dayton?"

"A little of both," Riley said, crooking her left arm out the open window and leaning against the door as they pulled around the corner and entered the construction site.

The view of the land still took his breath away. So much was riding on this. Riley had done the pre-construction survey a year ago while he had wined and dined the venture capitalists. It was the first time he'd looked to outsiders to make a project happen, because getting back to Belle Terre had been that important to him.

"What's going on with the bookstore owner?" Riley asked as they exited the vehicle.

He'd filled Riley in on the mysterious sale by Mr.

Lautner to an LLC by phone last night, so he completed the story now. They leaned against the hood of the SUV, their body posture nearly identical with crossed arms and their weight balanced on one leg.

"By the look on her face, I'm guessing you hadn't told her you owned LCB," Riley commented. "That sure is going to get in the way of you and her getting back together and living happily ever after."

Will again kept silent but could feel his face warming beneath her close scrutiny. He kept his gaze out toward the open land.

"Holy hell." She blinked, staring at him with wide eyes and a smirk to beat all. "You've already gotten together with her. What did you do? Jump her your first day in town?"

"It wasn't like that," Will countered, not liking the lack of conviction in his voice.

"You slept with her and took her bookstore under eminent domain all in four days. I hope you made the most of it, because you're never going to see the insides of those panties again."

Sadly, she was probably right. He hated that about his ex-wife. That and her ability to read him like a book. Some things an ex just should not be able to do.

As he thought about the error of his judgments the last few days, the familiar '92 LeBaron screeched to a halt near the entrance of the construction site. Chloe was hunkered down behind the wheel, but she didn't look at him. The doors opened and BeckyLynn and Vince piled out, followed by a younger girl of six or seven. She clutched a scragglylooking kitten to her chest with one hand and slid the other into Vince's grip. They all had garbage bags in their hands. Vince held a leash with a dog that looked to be a cross between a poodle and a Dachshund.

Will's Spidey sense prickled. He started toward the car, but Chloe peeled out as soon as the kids were clear from the doors. Will met the kids halfway, Riley on his left. "Hey, kids. What's up?"

BeckyLynn hung her head and avoided his gaze. "Mom said we were staying with you while she went out of town." She passed him an envelope. Tears glistened in her eyes. "But I'm guessing you didn't know that."

Will took the envelope and tore it open, pulling out a single slip of paper. It read, *I'll call.* He folded the paper and tucked it in the back pocket of his jeans. "No, I knew about it," he lied. "I'm just running late with work. Who's this pretty little lady?" Will asked, hunkering down to eye level with the youngest of the three kids.

"That's Malice," Vince supplied and Malice sidled closer to his body.

"Malice?" Will questioned, not sure he'd heard his nephew right.

"It's really Mary Alice, but it got shortened," Vince replied sheepishly.

BeckyLynn punched her brother in the shoulder, but it was without much strength. "Yeah, cuz doofus here couldn't say Mary Alice."

Vince pushed back. "Cut it out, BeckyLynn. At least she talks to me."

"That's the other thing," BeckyLynn gestured toward her younger sister. "She don't talk much."

Will reached out and scratched the kitten on the neck. "Hey, Mary Alice. I'm Uncle Will. That sure is a nice kitten you have there."

Mary Alice buried her face against Vince's shirt, covering the side of her face with her kitten so that Will was completely blocked from her line of sight.

Will stood and motioned to Riley's vehicle. "Bex, why don't you get Mary Alice buckled in the backseat and we'll head over to my place to get settled in."

BeckyLynn didn't hide the shock. "You mean you're going to let us stay with you?"

It was Will's turn to be shocked. "Of course. Why? What did you think would happen?"

"I figured we'd end up back in foster care like last time."

Will swallowed the lump of regret clogging his throat and studied his shoes really hard before he could find his voice. He looked at the two older kids each in the eye, one after the other. "That's not going to happen, Bex. Steele. I promise. You can stay with me as long as you want."

BeckyLynn and Vince looked at each other sideways and Will couldn't miss the disbelief on their faces. He wanted to be mad at his sister, wanted to yell and scream at her for putting that look on her kids' faces, but he couldn't. He'd abandoned her the same way she'd abandoned her kids.

The three kids walked past Will and Riley somewhat slowly, as if still suspicious of Will, but they climbed in the car without a word and buckled in like he'd asked.

Riley slapped Will on the back, grinning from ear to ear. "Congratulations, Daddy. It's two girls and a boy." Then she slid behind the wheel of the car.

Will pulled his seat belt tight, very conscious of the three sets of eyes boring into his back.

After dropping Riley off at the hotel where she and the crew were staying, Will took the SUV and the kids and hit the local furniture rental place in the next town over. He recognized the cautious way BeckyLynn and Vincent watched his every move, waiting for the rug to be snatched out from under them when things seemed too good to be true.

"Let's start with bedrooms. Bex, you and Mary Alice will need to share. Want to pick out what you want?"

Mary Alice didn't have the reserve of her older siblings, however, and quickly rushed through the store tapping her selections for her and BeckyLynn's room. Like any good teenager, Bex rolled her eyes at appropriate intervals and sighed heavily as Mary Alice chose a set of bunk beds decorated with fairies.

"Fairies? Come on, Malice. And bunk beds? Anything but fairies," Bex begged, but she ran her hands gently along the wooden headboard.

"What size mattress are you used to, Bex?" Will asked, trying to gauge the size of the room with the furniture before them.

"We shared a twin," she replied somberly.

Will swallowed the regret pushing at the back of his throat. "You and Mary Alice shared a twin?"

"No. All three of us."

The words set off a fire in his belly, and he focused on his youngest niece carefully inspecting the fairies painted across the headboard. He cleared his throat, trying to keep the anger out of his voice. "I think we can get you each a twin. The room's not huge, but it shouldn't be too crowded."

Will was finally able to convince Mary Alice to trade the bunk beds for two singles in white wrought iron and a set of fairy decals for her side of the room. They added a dresser and nightstand for each of the girls. Vincent proved a tough customer, carefully reviewing his choices before selecting a bedroom set in burnished silver.

In a little over two hours, they had a fully furnished

house. Will paid extra to have the furniture delivered the same day, and by nightfall the kids were sitting around the new dinner table eating pizza delivery. The furniture made the house feel more complete, Will admitted. There was still one thing missing, he realized, eyeing the set of keys he'd found on the living room floor after he and Lara had christened the carpet. One person he wanted around the dinner table with him.

While the kids finished eating, Will stepped out onto the front porch, looking out at the neighborhood homes and remembering the families that had occupied them when he was a kid. Back then, he'd been jealous of the idyllic lives he pictured behind the walls of these homes. He, Chloe and Junior had scraped by thanks to Junior's less-than-honest approach to life. That life, however, had a little too much pull for Junior, and he went from stealing to survive to just stealing. It didn't take long before he was serving the first of many stints in juvie, and not much later he graduated to state prison.

With thoughts of his brother on his mind, Will thought at first he was seeing things when he spotted the shadowy figure creeping out from Lara's backyard. He'd seen Lara and her gaggle of houseguests leave earlier. The windows were dark and the drive way empty, so he knew no one was at home. So who was the clandestine visitor?

Will whispered inside at BeckyLynn to call the police, then started down the stairs. Just as he rounded the corner to the house, the figure clad all in black caught his eye.

"Stop!" he yelled out, knowing it would likely be useless. He pulled opened the gate and ran toward the burglar, who lithely hopped over the back fence into a neighbor's yard, then disappeared into the dark shadows on the side of the house. Will started to follow, then remembered the kids, so he held back, though it ripped at some part of him to give up. By the time he reached the front of his house, he could hear the sirens wailing in the distance.

Bodie and his deputy arrived, and he and his men searched the house and neighborhood. Will retreated to his own porch where the kids joined him. The rest of the neighborhood gathered along the sidewalk. The officers were just finishing up when Lara drove up, the top down on her new Miata.

"What happened, Bodie?" Will heard her ask as she exited the vehicle, smoothing down her windblown hair.

She and Bodie stood talking, then they moved inside her house. Will ushered the kids back inside, resisting the urge to go to her. He'd never felt so pulled in his entire life, but he couldn't desert the kids their first night with him.

Lara was safe. That was all that mattered. He'd make sure she stayed that way.

Chapter Twenty

S unday night dinner, and once again Lara sat in the same chair at her parents' table, staring at the empty place across from her. Instead of thinking about Brian's absence, however, Lara was wondering if Will could fit into her family. Trying to breathe through the tension surrounding the table, however, she wondered what sane person would want to join this family.

Sally and Katie had taken their plates and joined the kiddie table in the kitchen. They spent all their time there anyway, Sally and Katie had informed their husbands, so they might as well sit where they were appreciated.

"At least we'll be dining with people who should be acting like children," Katie snipped before disappearing through the kitchen door, giving her head a snap that made her long ponytail flick like the end of a whip.

"You told me to hire someone, Katie!" Jimmy snapped back, and Lara guessed they were referring to the new clerk he'd hired for his sporting goods business.

"I didn't tell you to hire your high school girlfriend!"

Yikes, Lara thought. She and her father both shook their

heads, sharing a look of pity and humor at Jimmy's predicament.

"What did Bodie say about the break-in, Lara?" Paul asked as he put a second helping of lima beans on his plate, his appetite apparently not affected by his marital discord.

"Since the burglar had a key, it wasn't actually a break-in, but they did dig up my damn camellia again." She pushed the food around on her plate, fuming. What was going on in her life? She hardly recognized it anymore.

"Language, Lara," her mother chided, and Lara bit back another slew of curses.

She grit her teeth. "He told me to get new locks, which I had put on this morning. Nothing was taken. They just searched through Brian's office."

"Did Brian keep anything important there?"

"Not that I know of. He had his office in town, so I didn't think he kept anything at the house. I'll check his other office after the funeral."

"Lara, honey," Helen chimed in, and her monotone cheerfulness caused Lara to tense. "What do you have planned for after the funeral tomorrow?"

"Planned?" Lara stopped pushing the roast beef around her plate. "I don't have anything planned."

"Paul!" Sally yelled. "The kids want more salad!"

"Jimmy!" Katie screamed from the kitchen. "Your son needs to go to the bathroom!"

Paul and Jimmy grunted out an "excuse me" and tossed their napkins beside their plates as they scooted back from the table.

"But people will be stopping by the house," her mother said over the rising arguments in the kitchen. "Surely you have something planned."

"I really don't think people will be stopping by, Mom,"

Lara reasoned. "Besides, if Brian would have wanted an after-party, he would have planned it."

"I hear you and Will had your own party in Dad's study yesterday," Paul added sarcastically as he returned to the table, surly in his wedded non-bliss.

Lara felt her cheeks flame. Her father choked on a laugh and quickly covered by sipping his tea, but not before Helen grated out his name between clenched teeth.

"That Will always—"

"Watch it, Mom," Lara warned softly and Helen went back to eating. Lara never dared speak like that to her mother before, but the way she said Will's name, the disdain, the contempt, sparked something fierce and protective in Lara.

Jimmy sat back down at the table and resumed eating. He had a bite halfway to his mouth when Katie again screamed his name.

"Jimmy! Your other son needs to go to the bathroom now!"

Silent this time, Jimmy pushed from the table and disappeared into the kitchen and Lara couldn't help but wonder if they would see him again.

"You stay out of Lara's business, Paul Louis Caldwell," Sally added in a mom-like reprimand from the safety of the kitchen. Several of the kids started snickering and chanting "Paul Louis Caldwell" and no one bothered to hush them.

When did her family turn into the dysfunctional Brady Bunch Maybe they could do a reality TV show.

Lara returned her attention to her brother, a little dizzy from the various conversations being yelled between the rooms. "Well, I thought about going to my house, but the kids were still sleeping and I didn't want to wake them with the noise," Lara responded somewhat saucily to her brother's snide comment. Her mother gave both her and her brother the stink eye, which twitched a little at the corner, Lara noticed but chose to ignore it.

"Paul, Lara," her mother said shakily and picked up the bowl closet to her. "More cabbage?"

Paul and Lara stared at their full plates and said in unison, "No, thanks."

Not to be distracted, Lara continued, "And thanks to you, I will no longer own my own business after Thanksgiving."

"If you'd learn to be reasonable," Paul replied haughtily.

"I've been reasonable for the last ten years and the only thing it's gotten me is a dead camellia and a jackass for a brother!"

"Lara!" her mother said.

"Helen?" her father warned.

"Howard?" her mother snipped in unison with Sally yelling, "Paul!"

"Sally!" Paul hollered.

"Jimmy!" Katie screamed though her husband was in the kitchen with her.

"What did I do?" a clueless Jimmy shouted back.

"Looks like the gang's all here," Lara quipped and stood up from the table. "It was a lovely dinner, Mom, but I've got indigestion now, so I'm going home."

As Lara escaped, a sudden onslaught of tears rose from behind her. Lara wasn't sure who was crying, but at least it wasn't her.

Chapter Twenty-One

W ill had never felt like crying so much in his life. "Malice, honey, please," he begged his niece, who stood forlornly in front of the two doors to the diner's restrooms. She bounced from foot to foot, doing what could only be called the pee-pee dance and shaking her head vigorously. "I can't go in there with you. You can go in byyourself or you come with me into the men's room, but I can't go in the ladies' room."

"Need some help?"

Will looked up to see Lara peeking around the corner and, except when she was naked, couldn't think of a more welcome sight.

"Malice, this is—"

But Malice took the bull by the horns, grabbed Lara's hand, and disappeared behind the door marked "Ladies." Will sighed his relief and made his way back to their table after receiving more than a few questionable looks from patrons while he waited outside the restroom doors.

He sat in the booth, his arm draped casually over the back seat. Bex and Steele had disappeared shortly after eating, leaving him with the youngest and quietest of his nieces. She'd just stared at him while he finished his pork chop and sipped his coffee, not saying anything or even responding to his lame attempts at conversation with a six-year-old. But she'd been very clear when it was time to go to the bathroom and had presented Will with his first parental dilemma. Luckily, Lara arrived to save him.

Watching Lara weave through the tables with Malice's hand tucked securely in her own, Will was overwhelmed with the sense of things falling into place. He knew things were tough on her right now and he hated his part in all of that. She struggled to define her place in both her family and community, a place that she picked rather than one given her. Will admired her for sticking it out. It was so much easier to move around and avoid the kind of attachments that could pigeonhole you somewhere you didn't want to be.

He'd never really laid down roots anywhere, not even here in his hometown. Could he do that now? Could he somehow take the ragged ends of his family and make them into something secure? He knew he could if Lara was there holding the ends with him.

Rather than her usual ankle-length dresses or knee-length shorts, Lara wore a snug-fitting pair of jeans that really showcased her curvy hips and rounded backside. A long-sleeved, purple LSU shirt skimmed the waist of her jeans. He liked the change. Still conservative, but sexy as hell.

Malice scooted across the blue vinyl bench, still holding Lara's hand, so Lara took the seat across from Will. His niece handed her one of the three colors provided with the kid's menu and Lara dutifully went to work on the picture presented to her.

"Did I hear you call your niece Malice?" Lara asked as she shaded a palm tree in orange.

Will pushed his plate back from the table. He signaled to the waitress for more coffee. "Apparently Steele couldn't say Mary Alice and it got shortened. I'm starting to feel left out. Everyone has a nickname except for me."

Lara smiled and Will wanted to kiss the dimples in her cheeks. Malice handed Lara the blue crayon and Lara handed over the orange. "Are the kids visiting with you for a few days?" Lara asked, her attention still focused on the palm tree she and Malice colored.

"Maybe a little longer," Will answered and hoped his voice implied the delicate nature of the subject.

"There are plenty of kids on the street Malice's age," Lara said, her eyes stealing a quick look up to him that said she understood.

"I saw you walk over to your parents' house earlier, I'm assuming for the traditional Sunday dinner."

Lara rolled her eyes. "Yes. My family puts the fun in dysfunctional, so I ducked out early."

Her tone told him more, but she wasn't ready to share yet. Malice and Lara silently switched crayons again, Lara praising her for the excellent shading on the orange-and-blue palm tree. Malice beamed and Will wondered how Lara could communicate with a non-communicative child. She seemed in her element, aware of Malice's lack of speech but not worried about it.

The waitress brought over a cup for Lara and filled it, then topped off Will's. They talked in comfort, avoiding topics that would spoil the casual mood. His time in the Marines. The fact that she still wrote like she did in high school. His travels. Old friends.

Lara focused on her artwork with Malice, and it struck

Will again how right everything felt with Lara around. She'd never been far from his heart after he'd left Belle Terre, and now, she'd wiggled her way even deeper into his life and he couldn't imagine what it would be like if he was apart from her again. Whatever else happened, he promised himself, he would not leave her again.

Lara and Malice finished their coloring and Lara caught him watching. She smiled that easy smile again and he was lost. "I've got to go. Tomorrow's going to be a long day and I need to check on a few things."

Will knew tomorrow was the funeral for her ex. "If you need anything, just let me know."

"Thanks." She complimented Malice on her coloring skills again, then whispered rebelliously to the young girl. "I think you should order some dessert. They have great pie." She slid from the booth and slipping away without a backward look.

The emptiness swallowed Will before she disappeared from sight.

Chapter Twenty-Two

The wailing wall.

That's how Lara came to think of the five women who were her almost-ex-now-dead-husband's lovers. In the days since her husband's death, she'd learned more about them than she cared to know.

She knew them all from around town. One was on the Welcome Wagon committee with her. Another served on the city council with her brother and sister-in-law. Judging by the number of tears being shed, they obviously had loved Brian dearly. How Brian had managed to love them all...

Live by the sword, die by the sword, Lara thought.

From her front row seat, she studied the gaudy and ostentatious coffin Brian had picked out some years ago, the overhead fluorescent lights glinting off the shiny silver handles and highly polished metallic finish. She hid the smile behind her hand. It reminded Lara a little of the space ship from Star Trek.

"Hey, honey," her dad whispered as he took the seat next to her. He wrapped his arm around her shoulders and pulled her close, kissing the top of her head. "How are you holding up?"

Lara leaned into the solidness of his body, feeling so much like a little girl who needed her daddy that genuine tears clouded her vision. Contentment flooded her body, knowing that he would be on her side no matter what.

A week ago, she would have been mortified to be caught by her father in such a compromising position. Heck, she thought, a week ago there was no one she'd *wanted* to be compromised with. Now there was Will. Lara chastised herself for thinking of Will at her husband's funeral, but she couldn't get him out of her mind.

She smoothed her hand against the lapel of her dad's coat, breathing in the familiar citrus smell of his cologne. "I'm okay."

She sniffled and he reached into his jacket and withdrew a handkerchief. It was one that she'd cross-stitched his initials on when she was nine and needed a project for 4-H. She'd ruined an entire box of new handkerchiefs before getting this one right. "Aren't you going to get in trouble with Mom for speaking to me?"

She felt the chuckle vibrate his body. "I'm already in trouble with her. I thought I'd come spend a few days at your place. You have a nicer dog house."

"Oh, Daddy," Lara cried, hating the thought of coming between her parents. "I'm so sorry." She knew redefining her life would cause problems for her family, but she never expected this.

"You have nothing to be sorry about. Me and your mom...this didn't happen because of you. Your mom can be a little unmoving when it comes to how things should be. Sometimes I have to remind her that change is good."

"I never wanted to cause this kind of problem. I just..."

"Wanted something for yourself." He patted her shoulder when she gasped.

"And you're not mad?"

"Mad? How could I be mad that my little girl is a business owner? The only one I'm mad at right now is your brother for that low-down trick he pulled as city mayor. And on his sister, no less!"

He cleared his throat and fiddled with his tie, the nervous gesture familiar to Lara when her usually unflappable dad started to get upset.

"Don't worry about that," Lara soothed. "I'm not done fighting yet."

Her dad gave her a puzzled look, but she didn't elaborate. Her thoughts went back to the woeful sobs of the wailing wall seated behind her.

The city council treasurer proved the loudest, but the city development commissioner had her beat on quantity. Her brother's personal assistant had the silent cry down to a fine art without smudging her makeup in the least. Maybelline really could do wondrous things with mascara, it turned out. It was the loan officer at the bank who'd declined Lara's loan application and the parish deputy, however, that threw the first punches. Silicone, Lara found out, was amazingly resilient.

Lara couldn't help but think, *I went to a fight and a funeral broke out*.

The sheriff was called, a first in the hundred-year history of Slumber Haven Funeral Home, and Bodie and Jackson stood guard over the five women who sat chain-smoking throughout the service. The funeral home was a no-smoking facility, but no one dared mention that little tidbit of information.

It wasn't until they'd moved to the graveside that the first wreath went up in smoke and flames. As the mourners scattered like water dropped in hot grease, Lara sat alone in the vacated rows of chairs on fake grass beneath the overhead awning.

She barely recognized her life these days, but couldn't mourn the loss, much as she couldn't mourn the loss of her husband. Neither had fit her the last few years. But everything changed in the space of a few short days. Her life was topsy-turvy and she loved it. The adrenaline. The freedom. There were problems, she admitted to herself, thinking of the bookstore and her disintegrating family, but at least she was living.

Which brought her back to Brian and the havoc he'd created, leaving her once again to clean up his mess.

When the fire threatened to jump to a second arrangement, Lara stepped forward and knocked the burning cascade into the empty grave behind her husband's casket. The fire sizzled in the layer of water at the bottom of the grave, sending up tendrils of black smoke and charred petals.

Burn in hell, Brian, she thought bitterly. Her family stared at her like she'd stripped naked in church and danced a jig. Lara touched the neckline of her blouse to make sure all the buttons were still done.

She shrugged and asked, "What did you want me to do?" to the gawking crowd, but no one provided an answer.

"Mrs. Haley?"

Lara turned and found the very unhappy face of the funeral director, Mr. Crane, staring up her nostrils. At least his right eye was staring. His left eye focused on the wailing wall as they lit up once again.

Lara watched the overhead whorls of smoke braid together and wanted to conjure up some feeling of anger or jealousy for the women who'd stolen her husband away from her. She'd blamed her own inadequacies for Brian's roving eye but, heck, five women? No wonder the man had a heart attack.

"It's Lara," she corrected.

"Of course. Lara." The funeral director enunciated the name carefully and whipped out a starched hanky to dab at the perspiration on his brow. "What would you like us to do?"

Over the man's shoulders, she could see the gathered mourners, though none looked very mournful at the moment. Instead, they all resembled kids at the circus waiting to see what would pop out of the clown car.

Taking a deep breath, Lara took her seat. "Let's get on with it. Brian didn't like to be kept waiting."

The preacher said his words and Mr. Crane and the sheriff directed the mourners into a respectable and, thankfully, quiet line past the casket. Lara stayed in her chair as her family and neighbors and Brian's business associates filed past. No one offered any condolences. No one looked at her directly. Lara was just as glad to be ignored, because she was sure her responses wouldn't be family-approved. She wasn't even sure they would be family-friendly.

Lara didn't budge once everyone vacated from beneath the funeral home's little tent. Will broke the magic circle of space around her and sat down. Lara felt painfully aware of his presence, from the warmth of his gaze to the aching hole in her heart.

"You doing okay?" he asked, sliding an arm across the back of her chair.

Lara didn't even care that a few mourners were still hovering about the cemetery and would witness her and

Will together. Seriously, what else could go wrong in her life?

"I've had better days," she said with a shake of her head.

"And I'm responsible for some of that," Will admitted, laying his hand over hers and squeezing gently. "I know this won't help, but I love you." He touched his head to hers. "It's so easy to love you. It's the easiest thing I've ever done."

Lara focused on the touch, the steady pulse that beat in his wrist as it pressed against the back of her hand. The warmth of his cheek. She closed her eyes and felt her heartbeat fall into synch with Will's as if it were the most natural thing in the world. The two of them had tried to make up for fifteen years of wanting and waiting in four days. Maybe they were just destined to be at the wrong place at the wrong time as far as each other was concerned.

She leaned into his touch, letting it envelop her completely as did his love. Even if it was only for this moment. Lara had been lost in her life until Will found her. The love she had for him overtook her.

"I love you." The words weren't enough, she realized. She entwined her fingers with his, knowing her heart was as tangled with his as their hands. "Loving you is the only easy thing I've ever done."

He kissed her cheek, her temple, ran his fingers through her hair to tuck the loose strands behind her ear. With each touch his hold on her wrapped a little tighter on her heart.

She stared at her husband's casket and realized that she felt more for the man seated next to her after four days than she did for the man she'd been married to for ten years. What did that say about her?

"Things are going to get complicated," Lara said more to herself than Will. A plan of action formulated in her mind during the funeral and Lara turned over the last few details she would need to take care of this afternoon.

Will looked at her puzzled. "What do you mean?"

Lara pushed to her feet and grabbed her purse. Her car was still at the funeral home—she'd ridden with her parents to the gravesite—but the hearse still sat parked at the cemetery. Will's bike sparkled behind it in the light filtering through the overhead canopy of trees. Which would cause her mother more angst, riding through town in the hearse, or riding back to the funeral home on the back of Will's bike?

The bike won.

Chapter Twenty-Three

The only people to show up at her house after the funeral were her father and sister, respective bags and kids in tow. They turned the back den into a kid camp and released the kids. Conspicuously absent were her mother, brother and brother-in-law, but given the circumstances, Lara couldn't blame them for laying low. She loved them all dearly and hoped things would somehow work out.

Luckily, Sally could make magic with leftovers and takeout menus and quickly whipped together a buffet for the hungry crowd. The remnants of the feast spread out before them. Katie, it turned out, was a whiz with the blender and produced several pitchers of very potent margaritas. Apparently, the mix came with alcohol already included, but she topped off the pitcher with the last of the tequila in Lara's sparse liquor cabinet, not that anyone complained or even noticed. The three women sat contentedly buzzed around the kitchen counter as her father kept vigil over the children.

"You should definitely redo the kitchen. The décor in here sucks," Katie stated, waving her margarita at the offending décor. "The wallpaper looks like a funeral exploded." Her jaw dropped at the unintentional quip. "Oops, sorry."

Lara waved off the apology. "Brian's mother picked it out and made the matching curtains," she explained, refilling her glass, then topping off the glasses of the other two women. "And anything Brian's mother made was untouchable."

Her sister-in-law plunked down her glass. "That apparently didn't include her son!" Sally choked out on a laugh, her drink sloshing over her hand. Katie giggled so hard at that she started coughing as liquor-induced tears streamed down her face.

"You two suck." Lara had a hard time holding back her own laughter, however, and tossed a napkin at Sally. "Clean yourself up, drunko."

Sally grabbed at the napkin and dabbed at her hand. "Seriously, Lara. The man had five girlfriends. I thought Paul was insatiable."

Lara cringed. "Ugh!" she growled as Katie hollered, "TMI!"

"That's our brother you're talking about." Katie grabbed a quesadilla from the plate on the counter, then spun her barstool slowly, head lolling back against her shoulders as she bit into the tortilla. "I remember," she said around a mouthful of cheese, "catching you two in the mayor's office right after he got elected. Paul was, shall we say, *polling* his voters."

"Oh-my-gawd!" Lara buried her face in her hands. It felt good to laugh, to let the worries drift away on alcohol-induced forgetfulness.

Not to be outdone, Sally tossed the napkin at Katie. "What about you and Jimmy in Dad's study the night before your wedding? Your husband is, uh, very gifted, from what I remember."

Katie blushed crimson and saluted her absent husband with a raised glass. "Here's to well-hung men, even when they are clueless."

The three women's laughter echoed against the walls as they raised their glasses in mock salute. Lara's dad poked his head in the kitchen, thought better of it, and ducked out again just as quickly. More laughter followed his hasty retreat.

"Man, that office has seen some serious action over the years." Katie waggled her eyebrows at Lara. "And speaking of office action...Do tell about Mr. Kenner, sister dear. Is he as good as we all wondered back in high school?"

Lara kicked her sister's bar stool into a slow spin. "Don't you go fantasizing about Will," she warned lightheartedly.

"Oh come on, Lara," Sally agreed, propping her bare feet across Lara's legs. "That man is a serious piece of eye candy." She snagged the last cupcake and made a great show of licking the icing off her finger. "Please tell us it's not all show."

"He's a shower and a grower," Lara squeaked out before the other two women guffawed loudly once again at her confession.

"Too bad we have to kill him." Katie downed what was left of her margarita in a single gulp. "Can't have him tearing up downtown to build an AmeriMart."

"Here! Here!" Sally cheered, following Katie's lead and finishing off her drink.

Lara didn't feel as inclined toward murderous intentions. "Can't we wait to kill him? I haven't had sex like this... well...*ever*."

"Then we have to figure out a way to stop him," Katie

chimed in, wiggling her empty glass at Sally, who promptly re-filled it.

The plan tickling the back of her brain during the funeral sloshed forward in her tequila-soaked state. *How do you stop a construction project?*

"That's what I was thinking," Lara confessed, her mind churning a million miles a minute, whether from the alcohol or the thoughts of sex with Will, she couldn't say. "Maybe I can steal his bulldozer." Then, with a smile, she joked, "He does have a nice bulldozer."

Sally sat up straight in her seat but swayed a bit before speaking. "We could kidnap him and keep him chained in the basement."

"We don't have basements in Louisiana," Katie corrected, sipping her fresh drink.

Not to be deterred, Sally countered, "Of course we do, but they're called indoor swimming pools. Can we chain up my husband with him?"

"Yes we can!" Katie assured her. "Paul is an asshat turd-muffin for evicting his sister. His own sister!"

Katie and Sally clinked their glasses in agreement to Paul's turdmuffin status.

"Come on, girls," Lara prodded. "I need a plan."

Katie hiccupped. "I like the idea of tying Will up," she offered, then added, "Jimmy likes to tie me up when we go camping without the kids."

Sally and Lara gasped appropriately, but Sally leaned over and asked, "What type of rope do you use for that?"

"Focus, you two!" Lara slapped her hand on the counter. "Besides, I'd have to tie up the entire construction crew."

Katie shook her head forlornly. "I don't think we have that much rope at the store."

While Katie and Sally swapped bondage ideas, Lara

slumped against the back of the bar stool, studying her nearly-empty margarita glass. Thoughts of ropes and chains and bulldozers floated on her inebriated brain and filled in gaps to the plan she'd been hatching since the funeral.

It could work, she convinced herself.

"Incoming," Lara's father warned from the hallway, then entered the kitchen with Katie and Sally's youngest under each arm. The kids' faces and hands were covered in green and red marker. "Art class got a little out of hand."

The ladies jumped up and retrieved their respective child, continuing to giggle as they hastened toward the stairs.

"Hey, Sally," Lara called out suddenly. "Do you still have keys to Paul's office?"

"Of course. Why?" she asked in return.

"Just wondering."

Howard meandered into the kitchen, pausing briefly to press a kiss to his daughter's cheek.

"What's that for?" Lara asked and patted the seat next to her.

Howard shrugged and slid behind the counter instead. "Just 'cause."

Lara studied her dad as he stacked empty dishes and wiped down the counter. The gray was winning the battle against the dark brown hair and he'd foregone the comb-over for letting nature take its course on his balding head. There was still a sparkle in his green eyes and a sturdy, square set to his shoulders.

He'd always been the quiet one in the family, she realized. Lara wondered if he'd been quiet out of contentment or desire not to rock the boat. "Are you happy, Dad?"

"Always, sugar," he responded without hesitation, looking at her with a smile that warmed her to the core. "I've got three great kids, a son-in-law and daughter-in-law that I love just like my children, grandchildren filling the back room and a wife I love more than the day I met her. If I get any happier, I might just bust."

Lara felt tears spring up and she wiped her eyes before they fell. "I guess I'm jealous."

Howard put down the dish towel and moved beside her, folding her in his massive arms. "Don't be. Your time is coming. I know it." He released her, plucked a tissue from a nearby box, and pressed it into her hand.

"I wish I knew it as confidently." Lara blew her nose and tossed the tissue in the wastebasket.

"Will is a good guy. I shouldn't have let your mother intimidate you so much when you were younger, but I..." The words trailed off and he looked at her sadly. "Then you met Brian and I hoped Brian would make you happy."

"I don't know that I'll ever find happiness, Daddy. What if I don't?"

Her dad looked at her sharply. "Happiness isn't something you find or are given, Lara. It's something you make. You can't wait for things like happiness. You have to go out and hunt that sucker down."

Lara considered her dad's advice and leaned into the security of his embrace once again. Could she make herself happy?

"Then it's about to get a bit bumpy around here," she warned him.

"Good bumps just test the shock absorbers and our family has good shock absorbers. Trust me."

So she did.

Chapter Twenty-Four

Lara sipped the strong coffee from her travel mug, watching as the sun slowly stole the sky from the full moon still visible beneath the thin spattering of clouds. Layers of color shared the eastern horizon over the river, from the deepest indigo at the top to the faintest of pinks below, providing a backdrop to the silhouette of bare trees. The air was chilly and hinted of wood smoke and a dampness heavier than rain. She'd always liked this time of day. She called it the moment of infinite possibility, when absolutely anything could happen with the day ahead.

Putting her coffee mug into the cup holder on her chair, Lara adjusted the chain circling her waist. She then threaded the other end of the chain through the bucket of the bulldozer sitting on the back of the flatbed truck at the entrance to the AmeriMart construction site. She snapped the combination padlock in place with a sharp click and tugged on the contraption for good measure. Lara then grabbed her sign that read "LCB + Belle Terre unfair to small business" and settled into her lawn chair to await the arrival of the construction crew.

The idea came to her during the funeral, of all places. Watching Brian's five lovers should have inspired thoughts of jealousy and retribution. Instead, the women made Lara think of a picket line, and *voilà*, the seed of an idea was born. Last night's foray to Margaritaville with her sister and sister-in-law just cemented the crazy notion into a full-fledged plan of action.

When she left the house in the pre-dawn hours that morning, Lara knew she was about to throw gasoline on a fire. Rather than taking her usual tact and backing down, she was at least going to fight. Even if she lost, and she expected to lose, she would know that she'd picked a side and done her best. Losing her bookstore would not be another boxwood hedge in her life, a symbol of quiet acquiescence. If she was going to lose the bookstore, then she would go down in blazing glory.

Hopefully not beneath a chain saw, however.

The thing that saddened her the most, however, was losing Will. Somehow, she'd fallen back in love with him over the past few days. Maybe she'd never fallen out of love with him, she reasoned. While she hated the thought of relying on one-liners, *Houston, we have a problem*. They were on opposite sides of more than the proverbial tracks this time. Lara took a deep breath and let it out slowly.

Before long, the huge white SUV she'd seen pull into town with Will's ex-wife turned into the construction site and parked in front of the trailer. Riley stepped out of the vehicle, sultry even at seven a.m. with a hard hat squashing down her hair. It took only seconds for her and Lara's eyes to meet but instead of anger or shock, Riley threw back her head and laughed full out. Not exactly the reaction Lara was expecting. Riley retrieved a cell phone from the front pocket of her jeans and put the phone to her ear. Calling Will, Lara assumed, and something inside of her twisted at the thought of that woman talking to Will.

She had no right to be jealous, Lara tried to convince herself. She had an ex. Will could have an ex. Will could have ten exes. It's not like they had a future. He was stealing her bookstore, for heaven's sake. He was ruining Belle Terre. Will Kenner was evil incarnate, her brain reminded her. Now she just had to convince the rest of her.

Riley walked to the flatbed with the deliberate ease of a woman who knew men would watch her. Again, Lara tried not to be jealous, but it was hard not to feel something toward a woman who oozed that much confidence. She adjusted the chain around her waist, wondering if it made her hips look too big.

"Good morning, Lara," Riley called out as she climbed up the back of the flatbed. She didn't have any weapons that Lara could see other than a killer body wrapped in skinny jeans and a long-sleeved t-shirt that said, "The eyes are further up." Lara felt decidedly frumpy next to Will's ex in her boy jeans and flannel shirt.

"Good morning Mrs...Ms..." Lara struggled, wondering what Miss Manners would say in this situation. She crossed her legs and picked up her coffee mug, wrapping her hands around the cup.

"Just Riley," she filled in, her drawl neither exaggerated nor false. She removed the hard hat and shook her hair loose. She stood like a climber planting a flag at the top of a mountain, one leg cocked to the side, the hard hat tucked against her nonexistent hips. "I haven't been a missus in almost three years."

"Sorry," Lara said, taking a long slow sip of her coffee, letting the caffeine and vanilla hazelnut goodness seep into her brain. "How long were you and Will married?"

Riley moved to the edge of the flatbed as two more vehicles pulled in past the gate. She waved at the men who exited. "It took us a little over two years to figure out we made better business partners than bed partners."

"Business partners? So you own LCB with Will?"

"Not equally. He and I worked together, and when he started LCB, I came with him. When we divorced, he insisted I take a twenty-five-percent interest. It's my retirement fund. I figure I'll get tired of hanging with these bozos one day and living out of an RV and hotels."

More trucks joined the two others waiting near the trailer, and more men spilled out. "Must be hard being the only woman."

"Nah. You have to decide to be their mother, their sister, or their girlfriend. Since I'm about as motherly as Lizzie Borden, I try for the sister."

"I'm guessing you called Will," Lara prodded.

"Yeah. As soon as he gets the kids off to school, he'll be right over."

Chloe abandoning her kids to Will had been one of the topics they'd avoided at the diner yesterday, along with the bookstore and Will's construction company. As much as he struggled with his own abandonment of the family, this must have devastated him. A sliver of guilt nagged her conscience for adding to his troubles before she remembered what he'd done to her bookstore.

By now, the majority of the construction crew milled around the site, some taking her picture with their cell phones. The others just sat on the tailgates of their trucks with coffee and donuts like they were waiting on a movie to start.

Riley leaned back on her hands, watching the crew. "Do you know what LCB stands for?"

"Yeah, I think so." Lara flashed back to the night Will was driven from her life in the back of the sheriff's car.

"Did you know his crew is made up of parolees?"

She felt her jaw drop, but Lara quickly clamped it shut. "No, that I didn't know."

"Will's real big on second chances, so guys come to him knowing they'll get a fair shake. I can only remember one time when one of those second chances bit him in the butt. And he takes his responsibility to keeping the paychecks coming real seriously."

The thought weaved its way around Lara's brain. She wasn't surprised now that she thought about it. Will had come back to Belle Terre looking for his own second chance.

"He's also crazy about you, you know," Riley said. The woman had taken a seat with her legs dangling over the edge of the flatbed, her hands tucked beneath her thighs. "It wasn't until after we were married that he told me about you, but I knew then he'd always love you best."

Lara thought about that for an instant, warmed by the knowledge that Will loved her. He'd known her the best of anyone and still loved her. It was what she wanted. So why didn't the knowledge make her happy? Maybe because, once again, they were pulled in opposite directions by obligation.

"Will and I have never had the best of timing," Lara admitted, feeling the regret pull at her words.

Riley laughed again, not in a malicious or superior way, but in the way a woman does when she understands all too well. "Honey, love doesn't exactly wait for the right moment. It just sort of hits when it hits. Kind of like a hurricane or a tornado."

"Or an AmeriMart store," Lara deadpanned.

Riley didn't respond right away. Instead, she opened her

coffee and blew across the top, the steam making ghostly vapors in the morning air.

"Have you looked at the last three financial reports put out by the city?" she asked finally, taking a cautious sip of her coffee.

"Yes," Lara answered, remembering the difference between the revenue and expense columns. Paul told her at a family dinner one Sunday that something would have to change in order for Belle Terre to make the city budget for more than six months. If they couldn't, that meant a lot of people with no paychecks. People like Bodie and her brother.

"LCB Construction has a strong history of revitalizing struggling towns with the corporate strength of businesses like AmeriMart. Research shows that in the last three fiscal quarters, city tax revenue has decreased in Belle Terre. AmeriMart would contribute significantly to that bottom line."

"What about the increase in crime?" Lara asked, still not wanting to be convinced that AmeriMart could help Belle Terre. "Donnelley saw a five-percent increase in crime overall after AmeriMart came to town."

Riley nodded. "But they also saw an increase in population by twenty percent. The crime rate is actually lower when you look at it on a per capita basis."

As if on cue, Bodie LaBeauf turned his sheriff's car into the construction lot, followed closely by Will on his bike. As the two men made their way over to Lara and Riley, Lara couldn't help but squirm inwardly. Will's face was grim, his hands tucked into the pockets of his jean jacket. Bodie, on the other hand, barely contained a wicked grin and seemed more relaxed.

Bodie spoke first. "Morning, Lara." He tipped his hat

toward Riley. "Ma'am. I'm Sheriff Bodie LaBeauf." He extended his hand.

Riley accepted the proffered handshake. "Riley Kenner."

If Riley's name surprised Bodie, he didn't show it. "Seems we're going to have an interesting morning here."

Chapter Twenty-Five

Will gave Riley a half smile and nod as he ate up the distance between them, his attention completely focused on Lara. She looked like one of those LL Bean models showing off the latest fashions in mountain gear and cold weather survival. The models however, didn't share the same look of fierce determination, nor were they wearing chains and padlocks. If his insides weren't doing flips at the sight of her, he might be upset that she intended to delay the start of construction on the store.

Riley hopped off the truck with cat-like grace, putting her hard hat on and grabbing her coffee. As she passed between Bodie and Will, she said, "I'll go get the guys started on unloading the remainder of the equipment. I think you and Bodie can handle Little Miss Protest here."

Will scrubbed a hand across his stubbled jaw, realizing he'd forgotten to shave this morning as he'd scrambled to get the kids off to school. Luckily, all three school buses stopped within a block of the house, so he'd not had to deal with taking the kids to their respective schools on the back of his bike. He could continue to borrow one of the construction vehicles, but he'd need to get a car, because he didn't expect Chloe back anytime soon.

But that was a problem for later in the day. For now... now he had Lara.

When his attention went back to Lara, he found her watching him, a flowered travel mug of coffee clutched between her hands. Her curls were squished beneath a knit cap, tendrils escaping to spiral like curlicues of ribbon around her face. The look on her face wasn't exactly triumphant, but it did remind him of a cougar with a rabbit in its sights.

"I don't even know where to begin with this," he stated, more to himself than Bodie or Lara.

"Well, I do," screamed a voice from behind. Everyone turned to see Paul standing just outside their circle. "Arrest her, Bodie. Arrest her for trespassing or illegal protesting or *something*!"

Bodie crossed his arms across his broad chest and nodded his head thoughtfully. "That might run counter to Lara's constitutional right to peaceably gather and protest, Mr. Mayor."

"Besides, I have a permit," Lara added, waving a piece of paper in her hand like a flag at the Indianapolis 500.

"A permit?" Will looked to Paul and Bodie, who reached for the permit. "How did she get a permit without the mayor knowing about it?"

Paul groaned.

"According to section 91 of the city code, an application for a public gathering must be submitted to the city secretary," Lara provided, looking rather pleased with herself. She and Sally had made a midnight run to the mayor's office after getting the kids to bed, using her dad as a designated driver.

"My wife." Paul winced, his face red from more than the chilly morning air. Then it was if realization fired from within he lifted on his toes and pointed at Lara. "Sally forged my signature. Arrest her for that."

"I can't arrest Lara for something your wife did, Paul," Bodie countered.

"Besides, Sally is your legal proxy. You set it up yourself."

His raised arm fell limply to his side, his voice still trying for in charge. "You can't do this to me, Lara. You're my sister!"

"You stole my bookstore!"

"I didn't know it was your bookstore until it was too late. I had to find it out from legal."

"And how long after that did it take you to evict me?"

Will thought Lara looked rather pleased with herself, and although he couldn't forget that she was standing in the way of starting his project, he was rather pleased for her. He knew what it was like to want to succeed, to escape the narrow little world people created for you, and Lara had done it. Paul may have gotten the first word in this battle, but Lara had one-upped him just fine.

Score one for The Book Nook, he thought.

Honking horns drew their attention to the front gate of the construction site just in time to see a bright yellow van pull up with WKRZ emblazoned on the side in red flames. Will thought it appropriate since his day was rapidly going up in smoke.

He went back to looking at Lara who, even with her sign purporting the unfairness of his company, still managed to make his heart beat faster. Will sighed. Lusting after the enemy would get him nowhere.

"Uh, Sheriff," Will started, choosing his words carefully.

"This permit. Does it give her the right to protest on private land?"

Bodie flipped the pages of the permit and finished reading before he commented. "No," he started and Will and Paul shared a momentary sigh of relief. "However..."

Will really hated that word.

"This isn't private land." Lara again waved a piece of paper at the trio on the ground. "According to the contract between Belle Terre and LCB Construction, the land does not become property of AmeriMart until the completion of the build. Until then, it's city property."

Paul threw up his hands in defeat. "Is there anything my wife didn't steal from my office?"

"*Your* office happens to be in *our* home," Sally added, joining the growing circle near the flatbed.

Dressed similarly to Lara and carrying her own sign and lawn chair, Will concluded she was here to join the fun.

"And it's not stealing if you can't be bothered to pick it up from the dining room table."

Paul stiffened and drew back his shoulders. "You moved out of *our* home," he reminded her.

"I'm on vacation." Sally hoisted herself onto the flatbed and took a spot near Lara. She busied herself with setting up her lawn chair and her own sign protesting the fairness of LCB construction.

"You only work two days a week," Paul said snidely, and Will could see that was going to get him nowhere by the warning look on his wife's face. "What exactly are you vacationing from?"

"You," Sally snapped, then lifted her sign and began chanting, "Belle Terre unfair to female business owners," while pacing the length of the flatbed.

While Bodie and Paul debated the success and consequences of forcibly removing Lara and Sally from the flatbed, Will stepped closer to the truck and looked up to Lara. He gestured to the chain. "If I'd known you were into bondage, I'd have tied you up long ago," he said, trying for funny but failing miserably.

Lara didn't smile and Will could see the hurt and betrayal on her face. Knowing he'd put that there carved out a piece of his heart. He had made a promise never to do that to her, and he'd managed it in less than five days.

Lara sighed and lowered herself to the flatbed, legs crossed. "If I'd known you were the owner of LCB construction, I might have delivered the orange juice and Oreos with my Buick," Lara replied. She dropped her head, chin to chest. "I'm not going to apologize for this, Will." She looked him in the eye from beneath the curve of her lashes, dark half-moons against the pale curvature of her cheeks.

Will scuffed his boots against the tires of the truck, racking his brain for a solution to the problem before him. He'd met resistance before on projects, but he'd never wanted to stay around after the project was completed. If he didn't fix this, his reason for staying would no longer be a reason. He loved Lara, probably had since he was sixteen, and she loved him back. That would be enough for now. She'd taught him that the night at the lake all those years ago.

"I know," he finally responded. "I don't expect you to."

"What will this mean for you? For LCB?"

He panned the crowd gathered near the entrance of the site, seeing men he'd worked with for the last five years. Losing this contract could mean the end of LCB, but it also meant not being able to pay the crew. They depended on him. Their families back home depended on him to make payroll. He thought of Chloe and the kids in his life now in that galley of people who counted on Will Kenner. The weight of that pulled his shoulders down.

Will rolled his shoulders and let out a breath. "For now, it means nothing. A delay. We deal with those all the time and build in extra days in the schedule so we can still make our deadline."

"I won't give up," Lara explained. She looked out over the site, her eyes panning from Will to the growing crowd. "I can't."

"Neither can I," Will sad sadly. "I've got everything invested in this project, and not just for me. There are investors to consider. My crew." He leaned his chest against her shins, his arms folded across her legs, looking into Lara's face and feeling the imprint of it solidify on his heart. "I put everything on the line to get back here to Belle Terre. Now that I'm here, I want to stay. I want this to be my home. *Our* home."

"It is my home," Lara said stone-faced. "Or it used to be. I'm not sure I'll want to stay here anymore."

Will flinched inwardly at her words. "Wait a minute—"

"Last chance, boy," Lara repeated the sheriff's words from Will's last night in town. "That's what LCB stands for, isn't it?"

"Yeah." He pushed away from the truck and shrugged deeper into his jacket. "Just so you know, I'm not giving up, either. And I'm not just talking about the project. I'm not giving up on us. Don't *you* give up on us." He heard the desperation in his voice and felt it strangle things deep inside of him.

Lara shook her head, moving the protest sign from one hand to the other. "I don't see how we can get past this, Will. I really don't."

"Just promise me you won't give up on us."

"What should I give up on, then? My bookstore? This town?" Lara asked, her voice strangled with emotion. "You're going to be like everyone else."

"What's that supposed to mean?" He stood and pinned an arm on each side of her body. Anger singed the edges of his emotions, but it was an anger born of fear. Fear that Lara would once again be out of reach.

"You said you wanted to know me and I let you see that person, but now that I'm in your way, now that I stand between you and this project, you want me to roll over and give up."

Will drew back, wary of the edge in Lara's voice. "No... that's not what's going on here. I never said for you to give up."

"No, just change what I want so it suits your needs." She looked away from him and her voice was low and shaky. He remembered he'd said just those words to her. "Just like everyone else."

"Lara, look at me," Will pleaded. He could feel her shutting him out because his heart was about to pound out of his chest trying to reach her. "Please."

She swiped her hand across her face before she turned to meet his eyes.

"I love you," he stated so matter-of-factly he couldn't see how she could disagree. "We can work this out."

"I love you, too. But I don't see how."

And her words were like a bulldozer sitting on his heart.

Chapter Twenty-Six

For a town that didn't like change, Will watched in amazement at how much changed over the course of twenty-four hours. Picketers overran the construction site the morning after Lara started her protest. After WKRZ's first newscast with "Krazy Dave" announcing the picket by The Book Nook owner Lara Caldwell Haley, the Coalition for Order and Decency beat a hasty path down to the river front to join in the fray, waving signs that denounced The Book Nook and in particular author Angelina Williams. They showed with great enthusiasm several large boxes of said books and promised to burn the copies in protest.

Close on the heels of the coalition, the Louisiana Ecology and Animal Friends showed up with fliers and signs showing the white-tailed dwarf tit-mouse and proclaimed that LCB would destroy the habitat of the last mating pair in the state. And just to keep things interesting, the Cypress Covenant Co-op, which happened to be made up of Lara's ex-husband's five girlfriends, showed up to picket Lara for interfering with the economic recovery of the entire town, not to mention their own pocketbooks.

No, Will explained to the collection of microphones shoved in his face that morning from a myriad of news outlets from Baton Rouge to New Orleans. He didn't have anything against the white-tailed dwarf tit-mouse, but thought it looked a lot like the hamsters for sale over at the PetStop. And no, he hadn't read Angelina Williams, so couldn't comment about whether or not it was pornography but believed in the First Amendment and the right of all adults to enjoy pornography if they desired. No, he had no comment on whether or not he was one of those adults. Finally, he had no thoughts about the picketers picketing the other picketers because he was in construction and not abnormal psychology.

When he finally made it through the line of microphones and cameras, Will paused beside the deputy standing between his construction crew and the pack of onlookers pushing at the police tape. "Hey, Jackson."

The two men shook hands. Will wasn't used to looking up to meet the scrutiny of another but with Jackson, he found himself having to crane his neck.

Jackson looked out over the crowd, shoulders squared. "Will." He nodded to one group of protestors, their signs proclaiming the construction site sat at the nexus of an alternate dimension. "Looks like your fan club added a few members overnight."

"And I was hoping no one would notice the alternate dimension."

"Sure would make traveling easier if you didn't have to fight the airport security lines."

Will laughed. He liked Jackson, having gotten to know him a little as the man kept as much peace as could be expected. "Can I get you anything? Coffee? Chair and a whip?"

"Your ex-wife's number?"

Maybe Will didn't like him that much. He pushed his way into the construction RV where Riley waited with hot coffee. He thought about warning her about the deputy but knew better. Riley could take care of herself. Maybe he should warn Jackson instead.

Will slumped down on one of the cushioned benches and peeked through the vertical blinds at the construction site. Lara still sat in her lawn chair, chained to the bulldozer, with her sister, sister-in-law and father perched like guardians on three sides. He hadn't talked to her again. Or, more accurately, she hadn't talked to him.

He'd tried again on Wednesday after the crew went home for the day, but she ignored him. Her silence stabbed at him, more painful than anything else. At least if they were communicating he could try and reason with her.

"I hear we're going to make the national news tonight on Fox," Riley informed him, propping her feet next to him on the bench. She popped the last bite of a donut into her mouth, licking the icing off her fingers. "And they made a David and Goliath joke about Lara and LCB on the Tonight Show last night. Wanna guess which one we were?"

Will peered over at the box of donuts but had no appetite for food. "I'm guessing the taller one."

"Then you want to guess who I just got off the phone with in Montpeltier, Illinois?"

Will groaned. Montpeltier was the headquarters of AmeriMart. "Has Steve Weston called yet?" Weston was the president of Weston Ventures, the bankroll behind Will's project.

"Nope," Riley replied and slid a thick file across the table toward Will. "But Mr. Venture Capitalist did send these by FedEx. Says we have until Monday to start construction or he and his friends with money are withdrawing from the project."

Will pinched the bridge of his nose, wondering what an aneurism felt like and if it would be less painful.

"I really don't get it," Riley said, getting to her feet. "You'd think we were bringing the black plague instead of tax revenue. What does Lara have against a market square with markets?"

And like a flash of lightning, the idea struck Will. "That's it," he said and even to himself he sounded amazed.

Riley paused. "What's it?"

Will bounced off the bench, diving into the boxes of files stacked near his desk. "Where are the blueprints for the store?" He flipped open boxes and thumbed through the thick binders within. He fired off questions before Riley could answer. "Would you get me the survey reports for the land? Is the CAD program loaded on the laptop?"

Riley and Will spent the next thirty minutes finding the documents Will wanted, though he wouldn't tell Riley why. He just booted up the laptop and went to work, certain he had the answer to their problems. He just had to convince AmeriMart to radically change their business and the venture capitalists to trust his vision. More importantly, he had to convince Lara. Because it really only mattered if he changed the world if Lara was a part of it.

No problem.

Chapter Twenty-Seven

Lara stretched her arms over her head, feeling the tension knotted in her shoulders tighten down her back. She'd slept on the flatbed the last three nights in a popup tent her sister provided. Katie delivered a couple of nice kerosene lanterns and camp stove, a thermal sleeping bag and a little fold out table for Lara's first night of protest camping from Jimmy's store. Now on night three, the effects of sleeping on the unforgiving surface of the flatbed truck started to take their toll on Lara.

Sally, Katie, and her dad took turns getting the kids to and from school, not to mention dealing with soccer practice, play practice, karate practice, piano lessons, singing lessons, homework, supper, sibling rivalry and bedtime, then joined Lara for some meaningful sign waving.

Jimmy and Paul stopped by a few times to do some groveling sandwiched between accusations and arguments about the impact the separation was having on the children. Painfully but not surprisingly absent had been Lara's mother. Her father hadn't gone by the house or called, and Lara figured he was giving her some time and space for a reason. After all, her entire family had self-imploded in the space of a week. Helen needed some time to adjust to the new world order, because apparently the Caldwells needed therapy. Lots of it.

E ven now, with the sun setting over the Atchafalaya River across the street, Lara couldn't believe the commotion still buzzing on the lot of the AmeriMart store. She spotted several additions to the panel news vans outside and their associated on-site reporters waving microphones in the faces of anyone who paused long enough to gape at the collection of picketers. Her dad had brought her the latest edition of the Daily Gazette and her picture featured prominently on the front page once again. They'd captured her from an upward angle, her sign resting against the chair. The caption read, "Chained Resistance."

She'd thought things might get a little quieter as the week went on, but they'd actually gotten a little crazier. People stopped by on their lunch hour and when they got off from work, coming downtown to see firsthand the insanity that started simply because she decided to say "enough."

In spite of it all, however, the thing that distracted Lara the most was the fact that Will had not been by to see her in three days. She'd seen him come and go from the trailer that Riley worked out of, his arms overloaded with files and blueprints, but he made no attempt to speak to her directly. Lara was less than pleased about that. In fact, she was downright depressed.

She hated the thought of losing Will as much as she hated the thought of losing her bookstore, but it broke something inside of her to think of giving up or modifying her dreams like she'd done so many times in the past. Why couldn't she be loved simply for herself and what she wanted? Why did it always involve sacrifice of who she was at the core of her being?

A commotion at the front of the site drew Lara from the depressing path of her thoughts. Marching in a conga line, a torch-carrying Candy Barr led her Coalition of Order and Decency to the center of the empty lot, not twenty-five feet from where Lara stood. Each COD member carried a box, but Lara couldn't decipher the contents. Candy took up a central location and let her members circle around her, then she pointed with her flaming torch to a spot at the center of the circle. The members marched forward and began dumping box after box of Angelina Williams's books to the ground.

Infuriated, Lara tossed down her sign and quickly dialed in the combination to the lock at her waist. She jumped down from the flatbed and elbowed her way through the expanding circles of reporters, onlookers, and construction crew gathering to watch Candy's show.

"These books are a stain on the fabric of Belle Terre," shouted Candy, triumph and the heat of her torch pinkening the pudgy contours of her cheeks. She wielded the flaming torch in her hand like a sword. "It's time to rid our community of this smut once and for all!"

The COD members cheered, but most of the onlookers kept silent.

"You move that torch toward those books and I'll remove *you* from the fabric of this community, Candy Barr!" Lara yelled, finally breaking through the COD line. Her heart pulsed in her throat and every fight-or-flight instinct in her body hollered at her to fight.

"Don't you threaten me, Lara Haley!"

"It's Caldwell!" Lara yelled back, taking a stance between Candy and the books. The flaming torch haloed the women in shadows and light. "And if you think I'm going to stand here and let you burn my books then you've got another thing coming."

"We bought these books," Candy countered. "We can do what we want with them."

"Over my dead body," Lara growled, fists clenched in front of her. Every memory of being backed into a corner rushed forward in Lara's brain. Every defeat, every conciliation, every compromise she ever made in an effort to be non-confrontational bundled together and sparked a fire in the pit of her belly.

"Don't you mean over your husband's dead body?" Candy sneered, and the crowd around them gasped and *ooh*ed but tightened the circle around the two women so they wouldn't miss anything.

Lara stiffened her posture, narrowing her eyes on Candy. Candy had the good sense to take a step back. "I may have sold the Buick, Candy, but I still have my chainsaw."

"We're not scared of you," Candy stammered, looking to her co-COD supporters. She pointed the still-flaming torch at each member of her group. "Right? We're here standing up for our town. For what's decent." But no one stepped closer.

"Looks like you're alone, Candy," Lara challenged.

Candy's lips started to quiver and her chin trembled. She clutched the torch closer, the light encircling her body like an orange cone. "Well, so are you," she countered.

"No she's not," came a familiar voice, and Lara turned to see her mother move from the crowd, carrying a sign that proclaimed, in bold letters, "Protect our town." The older woman took up a place at the edge of the pile of books.

"Mom?" Lara couldn't believe it and quickly went to her mother's side. Tears of joy and relief and pride swelled in her eyes. "What are you doing here?"

"You mess with one Caldwell, you mess with them all," Helen Caldwell said with conviction, her feet planted shoulder width apart. Her face softened and she took Lara's hand in her own, and Lara could feel the love flow between her and her mom. They may not always agree, but it was good to know her mother had her back.

"Besides," Helen whispered. "I love Angelina Williams. That girl can write."

"*No!*" shouted someone from the crowd, and Lara and Helen turned in time to see Candy pitch her flaming torch toward the pile of books.

Shoving Lara out of the way, Helen lunged forward and swung her protest sign in a smooth underhand arc, connecting with the torch with a solid thud and sending it skyward. Every eye traced the trajectory of the flaming projectile as it tumbled end over end, skimming over the heads of the gathered crowd to plop down in the middle of Lara's flatbed campsite.

Then, in a scene that could have rivaled any B-movie comedy, they all watched as the kerosene lamps caught fire and fell to the side, one rolling into the pup tent, which rapidly went up in flames. So much for flame retardant, Lara thought woefully.

Someone in the crowd yelled for a fire extinguisher and to call the fire department, but most just moved back and watched the show continue to unfold.

Lara felt Will join her just as the fire spread along the base of the flatbed, leaping in long lines of old gas spills and oil spills that had soaked into the wooden supports over the years. Slowly, the fire circled the bulldozer until the entire orange body was engulfed in matching orange flames.

As the heat of the fire began to push the crowd back, Lara slipped her hand into Will's and squeezed. He squeezed back. She turned and stared into his eyes, shadows and light dancing along the planes and angles of his face from the red-and-yellow glow of the flames. Her heart melted beneath the scorching intensity she saw reflected in the endless darkness of his gaze.

A few of the construction crew ran forward brandishing fire extinguishers, but the growing flames proved too much for the devices. The fire leaped higher into the night, encircling the construction site in a dome of heat and light.

Will let out a slow breath, leaning his arm against Lara's shoulder. He tipped his hand forward and tucked a curl behind her ear, then traced the line of her jaw with the pad of his thumb. "Guess I'm going to need a new bulldozer."

Chapter Twenty-Eight

The fire trucks lumbered and groaned their way out of the construction zone, leaving behind the charred carcasses of the bulldozer and tractor trailer. The crowd of onlookers dispersed before sunrise, leaving Lara, her family and the construction crew alone with the wet, blackened mess. Only the news vans hung around the entrance. Boy, had they gotten more than they bargained for last night.

Standing near the spot where she'd held Will's hand last night, Lara closed her eyes, despondent. It was over, she realized with a despair so deep even her toes felt numb. Her protest had gone up in flames along with the bulldozer. She couldn't in good conscience continue along her current path. Someone could have been hurt last night. The entire river front could have gone up in flames, she acknowledged, thinking of the fire that destroyed the original buildings over a hundred years ago. She was just one person. Even though it killed something inside of her, she couldn't continue. The price was just too high.

Her family gathered the Angelina Williams books and boxed them back up. Now they stood huddled in the chilled morning air, waiting, watching. Lara bent over one of the boxes, picking up a copy of one of the books. The two people on the cover straddled a motorbike, the woman's arms wrapped around the man from behind. Confidence filled the woman's eyes. She knew she was going to get her happy-ever-after ending. Lara, however, knew her days of rebellion and kissing rebels were over. Will would build his store. Then he would leave. She'd go back to her life.

Looking up, Lara watched the news crews part like the Red Sea as Bodie maneuvered his sheriff's vehicle through the front gates and park. She slumped in on herself and gave in to the darkness for a brief moment.

Bodie exited the car, tugging his hat low on his head, and started in her direction. She wanted to sigh, to run or hide or just be someone else, anything other than the object of Bodie's attention.

Like a protective wall, her mom, dad, Sally, and Katie closed in around her.

"You can't arrest her, Bodie," Katie warned as Bodie stopped in front of them, arms linked hand over wrist in front of his body.

Sally nodded, waving her sign at Bodie. "Yeah, there are news vans right out there and they'll get you suppressing our protest and violating our civil rights."

"If you try and arrest her," Helen warned, "you'll have to arrest all of us. Besides, it was my fault the fire started. If someone's going to jail, it's going to be me." Howard took her hand, standing firm with his wife.

Bodie leaned back on his heels and smiled and punched one fist into the dent of his waist. "I'm just here to deliver news to Lara, not suppress or trample or violate. I save those for the weekends."

Lara pushed herself forward, taking the sign from Sally

and tossing it on top of the blackened ruin behind them. When Sally and the others gasped, Lara just shrugged her shoulders and turned to the sheriff. "Hey, Bodie."

Bodie scratched the back of his neck, casual-like, pulling at the collar of his shirt. "I had a talk with the...uh...other ladies in Brian's life recently, given the situation with his death and with the vandalism at your house."

She'd nearly forgotten about all of that, given the events of the last few days. "Did you find out anything interesting?"

"I sure did." Bodie moved closer to Lara. "Maybe we should talk in private."

Lara looked over her shoulder at her family, feeling closer to them in the last few hours then she had in the last twenty years. Will had made her realize that regardless of where you were, family was important. "No need. They're my family."

Bodie shifted beneath her stare, clearly uncomfortable with what he had to say. "Well, apparently Brian had been a little *neglectful* lately and several of his *friends* wanted to help him along in that regard. They'd each been feeding him the little blue pill secretly."

Lara rolled her eyes. Great. "So what does that mean?"

"His death will go down as an accidental overdose."

"And my camellia bush and the house break-in?"

"That's where things get a little interesting." Bodie motioned to the trailer where Will had again disappeared when the fire was under control. "I'd like to talk to you, Paul and Will about this all at the same time. Any chance of getting you to call a truce for an hour?"

Katie and Sally now flanked Lara and were quick to volunteer. "Don't worry, Lara," they assured her. "We'll stay put until you get back."

Lara fell in step alongside Bodie. They reached the

trailer just as Paul walked through the gated entrance to the site, and Lara saw his shoulders fall as he watched his wife. He ambled dejected across the site, arms heavy at his side.

Paul greeted her with a shrug and a half-smile. "I wish I knew what she wanted."

Lara shook her head. "I think Sally just wants to know she matters, Paul."

"Are you kidding? I'm a wreck without her."

"I'm not talking about things in the mayor's office or things with your campaign."

"I'm not either. I miss her. I didn't realize how much I counted on her. She's my sounding board and my compass and my...my...partner. I feel totally lost."

Lara wrapped her arm around her brother's shoulders. "Then tell her that, bozo."

"And you're such a good role model."

"That's completely different," Lara reasoned.

"If you say so." But Paul didn't look convinced. "I let Will down years ago and the two of you probably paid the highest price for my sins," he said contritely. "I'm really sorry, Lara. If I cost you the love of your life, I'm truly sorry. And the bookstore..."

Lara hugged her brother's neck, fighting the tears clouding her vision. "I have to believe things happen for a reason, big brother. Though I'm struggling to figure out what that reason is right now."

"Whatever I can do to help, just say the word. I may never be a state senator, but I'm still mayor, at least for now," he teased, sucking in his gut and thumping his fists against his puffed-out chest. He squeezed her into an embrace. "Do you know what Bodie has up his sleeve? He wouldn't tell me anything except to come over here directly."

"No clue. Let's go find out."

Paul and Lara stepped into the trailer. Blueprints covered every available surface of the desk, the kitchen table, and most of the walls. Coffee cups and takeout containers lay stacked in the sink and on the counter space and the faint odor of beignets filled the air around them. Bodie and Riley sat on the bench against the far wall. Bodie's arm was flung across the back of the sitting area, fingers drumming quietly against the window sill, his right leg crossed at the knee of his left. Riley glanced at the two of them briefly, but her focus was all on Will, who sat on the desk with a phone pressed to his ear.

Will and Lara locked gazes for what felt like an eternity and Lara's stomach flipped a time or two.

"Thanks, Steve. I'll finalize the blueprints and shoot them over to you and AmeriMart by Monday. We should start construction on schedule right after Thanksgiving."

And with those few words, Lara felt the last grasp of her strength give out on her. She spun on her heel to leave, but Bodie, Riley, and Will all shouted, "Wait!" before her hand touched the door.

She slowly faced Will, completely lost for an eternity of seconds. Bodie, Paul, and Riley disappeared into the periphery of her vision. Her attention was all for Will, the dark chocolate of his eyes, the sun wheat hair falling over his forehead, the jut of his hip as he slid off the desk and walked toward her.

He would get his store and LCB would give him the security he needed for his nieces and nephew. She'd had the acceptance he was looking for and now he would know the same thing and she was glad. When you loved someone, you were supposed to be happy for their successes, so Lara was.

She opened her mouth to say all of that, to wish him

well, to tell him congratulations when he silenced her with a kiss. And it was no ordinary kiss, no sweet hovering of lips against lips. This was the kind of kiss that ended epic movies when the hero and heroine finally made it past all the obstacles on the way to happily ever after.

When Will finally broke from the kiss, Lara struggled to find the air in her lungs to breathe, much less speak. Fortunately, that wasn't a problem for long because Will didn't give her a chance.

"Sit here," he directed and led her to the vacant corner of the desk. When she opened her mouth to speak, he kissed her again and Lara felt the blood pound in her ears and warm her face. "No talking. Just listen. Bodie, why don't you start?"

Bodie leaned forward, elbows resting on his knees. "My office did a little research, and it turns out the lawsuit filed on the property adjacent to the River Front Co-op's was filed by none other than Brian Haley."

Lara and Paul looked at each other, then back out to Will and the others. "Brian? But why?" Lara asked.

"Not to be indelicate"—Bodie nodded to Lara—"but Brian's involvement with the city business developer had its benefits. He apparently found out about AmeriMart's interest in building here and bought out the Cypress Covenant co-op two years ago. Only he put the shares in the names of his...uh...lady friends."

Paul palmed his forehead in understanding. "And when he died unexpectedly the women didn't have the authority to stop the lawsuit and sell out to AmeriMart."

"Exactly," Bodie confirmed. "They knew Brian had a safety deposit box but he'd told them he'd hidden the key."

Lara thought of the extra set of keys she'd given the police when they towed away the Buick. "Brian's keys. I remember putting them in my pocket after they returned the Buick, but don't know what happened to them after that."

"I do," Will said, scrubbing his hand across his jaw. "I found them in my living room after..." He let his voice trail off.

Lara felt the blush start at her toes and explode around her ears. "So they've been tearing apart his life to find it. And digging up my camellia bush," Lara added, thinking of the uprooted plant found with Brian's body. "They thought it was hidden under the camellia bush because that's what he died digging up. He probably never told them it was a part of the divorce."

"Yes. They also tore apart his office, but I'm guessing you hadn't noticed that yet."

"No, I hadn't been to the office since he died." She looked to Will. "Brian must have known about me owning the bookstore and knew I would never sell. Then he could come in with ownership of the adjacent property, sell out at an even higher price." She remembered the end of Will's conversation and her voice fell an octave under the realization that she'd lost. Even though she'd expected it, it hurt nonetheless. "And now you can build your store."

"Not exactly," Will corrected. "I wouldn't buy that property for a penny on the dollar."

Lara's heart swelled. "But if I won't sell and you won't buy the other property, how will you build?"

"Easy." Will turned around his laptop and tapped on the keyboard. A color rendering of the proposed AmeriMart store filled the large flat-screen attached. It filled the city blocks of downtown Belle Terre, an out-of-place monstrosity in the cypress-lined streets. "This was the existing proposal." He tapped the keyboard again and Lara cried out as the original picture morphed and evolved into something new. "This is the new proposal."

The new proposal showed the existing buildings intact with a charming series of replica architecture forming a walkway of stores and courtyards throughout the property. Will thumbed through a series of drawings showing the buildings up close, an interconnected flow of stores that would house AmeriMart and its departments. Parking had been added around the outer edge of the buildings. He'd created an outdoor walking mall that blended into the existing scenery so well that Lara wanted to cry.

"AmeriMart gets its new store, with some positive publicity about blending and supporting the existing infrastructure of its host cities without overwhelming the area. Lara gets to keep her bookstore. Brian's...ahem...lady friends don't make a dime. Belle Terre gets the revenue and taxes of new business and LCB now has contracts for three more stores just like this one."

Paul moved up closer to the monitor and began to question Riley about the new design, leaving a dumbstruck Lara face-to-face with Will. At her silence, however, his face fell. "Don't you like it? I thought it maintained the beauty of the area and..."

Lara launched herself at Will, flinging her arms his neck and burying her face between his chin and shoulder. Could this really be happening? Did her life just work out where she was going to get everything she every wanted? Her bookstore. Her family. Will.

"You were right. You did it. But why? You could have had it all by just buying the other building."

Will pushed her a short distance away, but still within the circle of his embrace. "Are you kidding? First off, I'd never have let those women make a profit after what Brian did to you, and even if I did buy that land, it would have broken your heart, and I couldn't do that. Not again." He tipped her head back with this finger, and she drowned in the flood of emotion. "I love you. I lost you once, Lara Caldwell. I won't lose you again."

This time it was Lara that kissed Will, sinking into the comfort of his embrace, feeling home for the first time in her adult life.

"I love you, Will. I hope you're ready for all that entails."

"Bring it on, sweetheart."

Epilogue

Lara pulled the turkey from the brand-new stainless steel double oven, her head swimming as the aroma of the slightly overdone bird filled the redecorated kitchen. She scooted the baking dish of her grandmother's stuffing aside with her elbow and slid the roasting pan onto the butcher block island she'd added last week. Once she cut off the burned part of the rolls, dinner would be ready.

Outside the swinging French doors, the doorbell rang and she could hear the swell of conversation as the kids yelled that they would get it, followed closely by a barking dog. She eyed the variety of dishes cluttering her counter, ignoring the not-so-pretty parts on some, and Lara couldn't help but smile. Nothing was perfect and she didn't mind one bit.

The kitchen doors swung inward and Will peeked around the corner. "I hear you've been cooking. Is it safe to enter?"

She threw a dish towel at him. "Just for that, you get seconds on everything."

He waved his hands in surrender and moved into the

kitchen, then wrapped them around her waist and pulled her close. Will lowered his head into the space between her shoulder and neck, nuzzling her ear with an appreciative growl. "Everything smells delicious," he whispered, then pulled back to kiss her.

Lara melted like butter on a hot roll, her hands sliding up his back to draw herself upward and into the curve of his embrace. "Good answer," she murmured against his lips.

"And dinner smells good, too," he smiled against her mouth, nipping playfully at her bottom lip while his hands cupped her buttocks and squeezed. Her body tightened and warmed and she wondered if love always felt like this, because if it did, they were going to miss a lot of meals.

It was Will that broke from the kiss, much to Lara's disappointment. "Your mom kissed me when I walked in the house just now."

Lara draped her arms around Will's neck and toyed with the back of his collar. "Apparently Paul had a heart-to-heart with them about what happened that night by the lake. Told them everything."

Will look startled, so Lara let it sink it for a second.

"What about his campaign for senator? If even a rumor of that kind of trouble gets out, he could be finished before he starts."

"He and Sally are talking it over. He doesn't have to file his intent for a few more weeks. Besides, my family can do some damage to gossipers. Who'd go up against that?"

Will rested his forehead against hers and Lara felt the love flow between them. "Your family really is amazing."

"*Our* family," she reminded him as he bent down to kiss her, letting his mouth move against her while his body did the same. "There are people waiting for food," Lara said without much conviction and swept her tongue against his.

"Takeout," Will replied, pushing her back until her backside rested against the counter.

With a quick peck on his cheek, she wiggled from his arms. "I warned you. I come with accessories. Like family."

He pulled her back into his arms and the look on his face—one of contentment and love and knowing that you were right where you were supposed to be—mirrored her own tidal wave of emotion filling her heart.

"I wouldn't have it any other way."

They each grabbed some dishes and started the parade of food into the dining room, where family filled every nook and cranny of available space. The kids ran around everywhere, some showing off animals to Bex and Malice while others taught Steele the finer points of Xbox basketball. If there was a dividing line between the families today, she couldn't see it.

"Dinner's served," she announced.

Jimmy, Paul, and her dad jumped up and started rounding up kids while Sally, Katie, and her mom helped carry out the remaining dishes of food from the kitchen. Will joined the other men and directed his nieces and nephew, their mouths agape at the food and people bustling about, to the card tables around the rooms serving as kid tables.

As Lara watched the insane chaos swirl around her like a vortex, her mind whispered the word "home" and she realized that she was. However crazy, however dysfunctional, however nosey, this was her family. She couldn't be happier. Her dad was right. Happiness was what you made, not what you were given. She'd made her choices and whatever consequences had developed had led her here. To this place and time. With this man and this family.

"Hey, kids," her father yelled over the din of noise. "Let's put the animals away for dinner."

A collective "awwwwwww" rose from the kids. Sally's oldest boy stepped forward with his hamster clutched in his hand. "But Granddad, Clinton can sit real still," he assured, and put the hamster on the table. "Watch."

Every grown up shouted "no" as the child let go of the animal and startled poor Clinton, who took off like a shot, weaving through the dishes and glassware lining the table. Hands shot out from all directions to corral the furry bullet.

Steele, who was holding Malice's kitten, screamed in pain as the kitten dug its claws into his shoulder and leapt like a gold-medalist gymnast onto the table, landing feet-first in the green bean casserole. Jimmy and Paul grabbed for two of the dogs who prepared for launch but missed as the canines jumped up onto the table, even the Dauschoodle.

They barked and followed the kitten, who followed the hamster, who blazed a trail through the dinner ware, knocking a carafe of wine into a twirl fit for a game of spin-the-bottle.

Screams and tears and giggles melded together as paws and claws scrabbled to get traction on the polished surface of the table. The turkey spun to the floor and dishes rained down like hail. The hamster disappeared under the couch and the kitten and dogs got scooped up by wide-eyed children.

After the lids and dishes spiraled to a stop, no one moved. Not a single child. Not an adult. And no sound escaped the stunned crowd either.

It was Malice that broke the silence, peering over the edge of the couch with a stack of papers clutched in her hands. "Uncle Will, what's a purple-headed pulsing rod of love?"

Lara stepped over the mangled turkey, around the puddle of green beans, and finally hopped lightly through the minefield of spilled rolls. "Oh yeah, I'm Angelina Williams." At Will's stunned expression, she took his hand and leaned over to kiss him. "Let's go out to eat."

THE END

Thank You For Reading

Reviews are the lifeblood of an author. Please consider leaving a review on any of your favorite review sites.

If you enjoyed *Sex and Insensibility*, keep reading for a sneak peek from book two in the Hearts of Louisiana series, *Second Chance Romance*.

Subscribe to the newsletter at www.AuthorMaggiePreston.com for release day information, prizes, and more!

Second Chance Romance

HEARTS OF LOUISIANA, BOOK TWO

Second Chance

Romance

CRIME SCENE - DO NOT CROSS - CRIME SCENE - DO NO

MAGGIE PRESTON

Chapter One

Riley Kenner pushed through the glass doors and into the crowded lobby of the bank, stumbling back as she was shoulder-checked by a harried Santa trying to escape a flash mob of kids with wish-list fever. The bearded fat man's eyes widened as they met with Riley's, but they clouded with fear and darted away as the kids zeroed in on their target. He gasped, a *huh-huh-huh* sound, and careened down Main Street's boardwalk.

She could relate.

She'd split from her construction crew, leaving them to find lunch with the rest of the after-holiday shoppers. Maybe she'd celebrate with a stop at the bookstore before grabbing a slice of pie from that little diner a few doors down. Her mouth watered at the prospect, both from the thought of the pie and from picking up the new Angelina Williams book she'd seen in The Book Nook's storefront window. She'd rejoin the crew as soon as she got the cashier's check. If she could remember how to sign her name.

It was finally happening. The not-very-jolly old Santa had nothing on her when it came to fear and uncertainty.

Reaching the bank counter, Riley scribbled the information on the withdrawal slip, pulling in big gulps of air, releasing slowly, then repeating. She walked toward the bank teller with to-the-gallows slowness, preparing herself to withdraw the money earned with her blood, sweat, and hard-earned calluses.

But it would buy her a house.

A home.

A place for her to find and to bring home the rest of the brothers whom she hadn't seen since she was ten. She'd found her oldest brother just last year. He'd helped her put the plan into action, and now it was all about to work out.

"Welcome to Bayou Savings and Loan." The teller's robotic greeting matched her plastic smile. "How can I help you?"

"I had some money transferred here on Wednesday from an investment account. I'd like to make a withdrawal." With shaky fingers, Riley slid the withdrawal slip across the counter before pulling out her driver's license from the pouch on her tool belt. "Cashier's check please, made out to Bergeron Estate and Auction."

Riley's nerves jangled like high-powered electrical wires. She fiddled with the tools hanging from the tool belt at her waist, wishing she'd left it in the truck, but its weight reminded her of what it had taken to put this money together.

Sixteen years.

She'd pulled out a hefty chunk of her life savings before Thanksgiving for the auction this past Saturday, knowing with the long holiday weekend the bank would be closed. The auction house had required ten percent earnest money to even bid on the property and that was a lot of zeroes. The unfinished house with thirty acres was appraised at almost a million dollars, but she'd gotten it for less. More people were interested in Black Friday deals than the property auction in Baton Rouge, so she'd been the only bidder.

And now the house was hers.

She'd sent her brother a message after the auction to transfer the rest of the money, so she could finalize the sale as soon as possible. She had until New Year's Eve but didn't want to wait that long. Her search for her missing brothers had been slow, but things were starting to fall into place thanks to those DNA testing and ancestor websites.

"Ummm, Mrs. Kenner?" The clerk worried her bottom lip between her capped teeth.

"*Ms.* Kenner." The correction automatic to Riley, like breathing. She really needed to go back to her maiden name, especially now that her ex was with someone new here in Belle Terre. But the memory of childhood taunts over the name's pronunciation, Fontenot, pricked her pride still.

Riley Fun-to-know...not!

"*Ms.* Kenner," the teller dutifully repeated. "That investment account was closed."

Riley's brain stumbled over the words. "Say that again."

The teller slid the withdrawal slip back toward Riley. "The investment account? It's empty. There was no transfer. You emptied out the account on Wednesday with your withdrawal, and the account closes automatically after seventy-two hours with a zero balance."

She'd tracked the withdrawal slip with the intensity of an eagle who'd spotted its dinner, but she didn't swoop in and snatch it. Riley's throat constricted, allowing only the tiniest slice of air to wend its way through. This was a simple misunderstanding. "The transfer was initiated *from* my investment firm on Friday. The money should be *here* today."

"It's not." The teller's expression tightened; the fine lines not quite hidden beneath too much make-up as her nails clicked against the keys. "The originating account was closed. The transfer never completed."

Riley's mouth went full-of-sawdust dry. Her chest tingled beneath the constricting of her ribs.

"That can't be right." Riley pulled out her phone, quickly logging into the mobile app for her investment account. Zero balance. That meant the money should be in her savings account.

Sixteen years of saving.

Sixteen years of waiting.

This could be easily fixed. Like a flat tire or a marriage where he still loved his high school sweetheart. "Can you look again? Maybe the transfer is still in process."

"I don't need to look again, *Ms*. Kenner." Ice crusted the words. "I can see it right here. The system would show a pending deposit if one existed. It shows the transfer cancelled due to insufficient funds."

Insufficient funds?

"No, no, no." The heartbeat in her chest hardened like quick set cement. "But—" Her hand landed on her waist to steady her. "I have a receipt from the ATM. I checked the balance on Friday." She blurted the words, and the teller took a step back.

Riley fumbled with the bag resting on her hip. She'd stuffed the receipt in her tool belt. "The receipt shows the investment account balance." She slapped a tape measure on the counter and reached in again. Panic nipped at Riley's nerves, her normal self-control tipping over the precipice. "It's here somewhere." *Breathe. Breathe.* "Just wait."

"Ms. Kenner..." The teller backed up again, and a slender man in a suit looked down his nose in her direction.

"There's some mistake." Her hammer came next, filling her palm with a comfortable familiarity that grounded her in the uncertain quicksand of the moment. Gasps ping-ponged behind her. Bodies shifted, shuffled, shushed.

"There was almost a million dollars in that account and that kind of money just does not disappear!" Riley leaned forward, reaching with her other hand for the withdrawal slip she'd written just seconds before her life fell apart.

That was when the teller's eyes saucered, her mouth opening in cartoonish-slow motion. Her scream, however, echoed in high definition.

The bank's alarm sounded a split second later.

Chapter Two

Technically, Riley comforted herself, she wasn't under arrest. The handcuffs were for her protection. At least, that's what the sheriff said.

"Are these the latest fashion trend in Belle Terre?" She clanked the handcuffs currently biting into her wrists against the chair where she'd been unceremoniously plopped. "What every innocent person under arrest is wearing for the holiday season."

Two dozen sets of eyes studied her in the bank's lobby—from a safe distance —their judgment washing over her like a bucket of nails dropped from the roof of a skyscraper.

"You're not under arrest." The sheriff's tone was clipped, but his ocean-blue eyes read like calm waters. His eyes dropped to the cuffs, while his body remained unmoving. "Those are for your protection." He paused. The crinkle of a smile he failed to hide lifted one corner of his mouth, and he added. "And ours."

"I didn't see anyone else getting tackled to the ground by a wannabe Saints defensive lineman." Frustration hissed from between her lips like steam from an overheated pressure cooker as she eyed the security guard standing over her shoulder. "I did *not* threaten that woman. You didn't have to handcuff me." Riley focused on the twinkling lights of the massive Christmas tree in the lobby, thinking calm thoughts. Very calm thoughts.

It didn't work.

She'd been in handcuffs before, deservedly so at the time, and swore it would never happen again. She'd kept that promise since her eighteenth birthday.

"And no one had to pull the alarm. There's a perfectly reasonable explanation for all of this."

But no one was listening, especially not Sheriff Sexy McDimple a.k.a. Jackson Guidry. They'd crossed paths before Thanksgiving, when her ex's girlfriend took over the construction site and chained herself to Riley's bulldozer. Thanks to a little *mishap*, it had gone up in flames. The bulldozer; not the girlfriend.

The sheriff leaned his impossibly long body against one of the lobby's columns, and Riley looked up to see if it would crumble under his weight. Not that the man was fat. Not a single ounce of fat would dare take up residence on that body. Though she wouldn't blame anything that wanted to stick close.

Based on the hungry looks of several women in the bank's lobby, she was sure he had more than ample opportunity to work off any extra calories.

He tipped his chin in her direction, fortunately oblivious to the wandering of her mind on his fat content. "I'm sure there *is* a reasonable explanation, Ms. Kenner. That's why I'm here."

Riley took a moment to watch the tall leanness of Jackson stand there and breathe; she could no more pull her eyes from him than she could fail to admire a Picasso or the perfect alignment of a platform frame when it came together on a building project.

"I thought maybe the bank needed an extra support column."

Another irritating twitch tugged at the corner of Jackson's mouth and broke the spell.

"Have you always been this annoying?" She didn't remember the smirk being so irritating, or so damned intriguing, when she'd first met the badge-wearing behemoth before Thanksgiving. And how had she missed that dimple in his left cheek?

"According to my sister, yes."

The drawl coated her like warm chocolate over toasted marshmallow.

His gaze slid to the bank doors, then to the star pinned to his chest, before finding Riley again. "But things were pretty hectic the last time we came face to face. Protesters, national TV coverage, and burning bulldozers tend to distract people from noticing the little things."

Judging by the myriad of faces staring at her from the bank lobby, so did bank alarms at the savings and loan.

Riley sighed, her eyes locking with JJ, her second in command on the construction site. He and another member of the crew, Noe Tam, had come running when the alarm sounded, pushing into the bank when others were rushing to escape. Noe stared daggers at the sheriff and Riley inclined her head toward JJ, who pulled Noe from the bank and back outside.

At least they wouldn't be witness to any more of her humiliation. This was not her life. She was used to being in charge. She was used to being the voice of calm. She was used to being able to ignore hunky men other women found irresistible. On a construction site, testosterone was as prevalent as two by fours.

"Sheriff Guidry." The bank manager's voice dragged Riley's attention back to her own unfolding drama as he joined them in the center ring of her life-circus. The fastidious man adjusted his tie with a little more care than it needed as his posture relaxed a notch below DEFCON I. "I didn't think you'd need to save us a second time this year."

The good sheriff winced, an almost imperceptible tightening around the eyes. The comment confused Riley while the sheriff seemed content to ignore it. "I'm still just Officer Guidry, Mr. Michel. Now, about the alarm?" Jackson turned his attention to the teller.

"She had crazy eyes, sheriff," the woman cowering behind the bank manager offered, peering out as if Riley were taking aim with a sniper's rifle. "And she pulled that hammer like she wanted to *bash* something."

"I was just taking my hammer out of my tool belt to get to my receipt." Riley dropped her chin to her chest, the hopelessness of the situation a weighty thing. "It's all a misunderstanding."

"She withdrew all her money on Wednesday but doesn't remember doing it."

"I remember the withdrawal!" Riley jerked up her head and yanked against the restraints, grimacing as the steel scraped against her wrists.

The gawking crowd took a collective step back from their vantage point just ten feet away from her spot at center stage of the action. A small step, she noted, so they wouldn't miss anything. Entertainment must be scarce in the sleepy little town of Belle Terre, Louisiana. She'd liked that about the town when she first visited just six months ago on a survey trip for her employer, LCB Construction. It was part of the reason she decided to stay in the area.

Only she didn't want to be the entertainment.

She continued, trying for calm. "There was just supposed to be more money in there today. Another transfer."

The good sheriff just stared at her; his arms crossed as he stood guard over her chair in the middle of the lobby.

"And after March—" the twitchy-fingered teller continued, narrowing her gaze suspiciously on Riley.

"I wasn't even here in March." Riley hated that she needed to defend herself. Hated even more that no one seemed to be paying attention to her defense.

"We get it, Tabitha." Mr. Michel consoled the woman, patting her shoulder like one would a poodle that had done an old trick. "You were just being cautious."

Sheriff Guidry stepped toward the bank manager, his arms falling loosely to his sides. "I took a look at the closed circuit video you provided, and she didn't actually threaten anyone with the hammer. Just pulled it from her belt." He pulled a set of keys from a pocket on his utility belt. "Did she do anything else that could have been perceived as threatening? Verbal threats? Physical threats? Even a scowl like the one's she's wearing now?"

"Hey!" Riley chimed in, tired of being talked about like she wasn't sitting there handcuffed to the chair. "I don't scowl." She purposefully softened the scowl tightening her face when a nearby toddler cowered behind his mother's legs.

Guidry scrubbed a hand across his jaw, back over his ear, keeping his head down.

But she saw it. There was the damn smirk again. How could he find anything remotely smirkable in this situation?

It was disastrous to say the least. Her money was missing. Her life's savings. Was anyone interested in that?

The teller shrugged. "I guess not."

Her words answered Riley's silent question as well. Riley sighed, dropping chin to chest.

Sheriff Guidry bent to remove the handcuffs, a not unpleasing waft of musky cologne surrounding him if Riley wanted to notice that sort of thing.

Which she didn't.

She jumped to her feet the instant the cuffs were off, rubbing her wrists and her wounded pride.

The bank manager stiffened his spine and squared his shoulders. "Nonetheless, the account appears closed."

"A million dollars doesn't just disappear." The big fat zeroes on the new balance receipt they'd shown her shot bullet holes in her soul. "There's just no way both accounts can be empty." Maybe if she kept saying it, it would become true.

She'd set it all up with her brother before the holiday, knowing he'd be busy with family. A wife, house in the suburbs, two point two kids. They probably even had a dog. A family she'd not been ready to meet. She blamed it on her travel schedule with the construction crew, but in truth, Riley had trouble being a part of groups, always feeling the outsider.

The bank had been closed, but Ricky had assured her the transfer could be initiated over the holiday—it was all just an electronic movement of numbers the way Riley understood it. The balance was due to the auction house at closing on New Year's Eve or she forfeited her down payment. Not to mention losing her dream house.

And her dreams.

"I assure you, Ms. Kenner," Mr. Michel sing-songed the

words with the calming tone of a hostage negotiator. "The account is empty. Zero balance. Closed. As of Sunday at..." He consulted a piece of paper in his hand. "Four-fifty-eight p.m. when the wire transfer was cancelled. Your savings account was closed at start of business today."

She propped her hip against the bank kiosk, her knuckles a shade paler than the crinkled receipt laying at her fingertips. Panic swelled in her chest, lodged at the base of her throat like a sticky lump of quick set cement.

"There has to be an error with the transfer then. The money was all there last week. I made a successful transfer before Thanksgiving. The rest was due to show up today. I need that money." Her voice pitched high on the last few words. From the corner of her eye, she watched the bank patrons start to edge toward the door.

"You need to remain calm, Mrs. Kenner." The gravelly voice of the sheriff with its deep bass interrupted her meltdown.

"*Ms.* Kenner." Riley pivoted sharply in her steel-toed boots, raising one finger to jab in the direction of the sheriff's nose. Only she hit him mid-chest level. A very broad chest only a hairbreadth away as it turned out. "And no woman in the history of the world has ever calmed down when being told to calm down."

"I wasn't asking you to calm down," he said, calmly. Dammit. "Just reminding you to be calm."

She tilted her head back to meet his cool scrutinizing gaze. *Damn, he's hot*, her libido kicked in. Her frazzled nerves squashed the temporary insanity of attraction. She punched her fists into the curve of her waist. "I am calm! Do you think I yell like this all the time?"

"My gut tells me yes."

The barely contained smirk—that was the only word for

it, she concluded, and it warmed things inside of her she didn't want warmed right now—brought out the dimple in his left cheek again. Didn't he get what was going on? Maybe the air really was too thin when you topped out over six-and-a-half feet.

Plus, she didn't like being one-upped in the sarcasm department. She took a step back to reclaim some of her personal space. "What does your gut tell you about what I'm gonna do next?"

He smiled, but it wasn't for her. "Keep making a scene until you get the answers you want."

Riley followed the direction of his gaze to a woman off to the side helping the baby on her hip wave at Sheriff Guidry. He waved back, tugging at the knot of his tie. A jab of curiosity—nothing more than that, Riley assured herself—hit her center mass.

"Perhaps this instance is nothing more than a...misunderstanding," Mr. Michel conceded, and reluctantly at that if the tight moue of his mouth was any indication.

Riley's hands launched from the perch on her hips, palms up. "A mis—"

Officer Guidry held up his hand, and Riley, to her own surprise, stopped mid-sentence, letting his Yoda-like powers silence her protest.

"You disagree with that, we know." The officer turned his attention to the bank manager. "Ms. Kenner needs some help, however, resolving the issue with her account and the transfer."

"Certainly, *Officer* Guidry." Mr. Michel stiffened his spine yet again and swept a hand toward a high-walled cubicle in the right corner of the bank. As he passed Riley, he nodded his head toward the officer and shot her a look that said, *He's watching you*.

Pissed, Riley turned to follow Mr. Michel and felt the officer's hand fall casually to the center of her shoulders. The jolt of heat surprised her. She leaned back instinctually, letting the weight of his hand guide her when she didn't need it, which surprised her even more. Apparently, she'd lost all her money along with her ability to walk unaided.

"You two look like you expect me to blow up a bulldozer or something."

Mr. Michel paled, and Riley wondered if he was going to pass out. The officer's smirk deepened.

She groaned inwardly at the stupidity of the remark. Her brain could only handle one surprise at a time. Possibly losing her life's savings—her future, her security, her ability to protect her family when she got them back, everything she'd worked damn hard to build the past sixteen years—definitely counted as a surprise. Some would even call it a shock. That was it. She was in shock. She needed fluids. A warm blanket. Maybe a warm body would do. The officer could definitely fill that last role, her libido suggested, and her frazzled brain thought of telling it to shut up, but she didn't mind so much this time around.

Damn, she was screwed.

Chapter Three

J ackson Guidry recognized the desperate edge of panic when he saw it. He'd been up close to people with similar looks on their faces when they made really bad decisions, flashing back to the bank lobby only eight months ago. It was a day that had changed his life. He'd avoided responsibility for the past ten years. He still wasn't sure if taking the job as deputy had been the right thing to do.

However, when Riley had rolled into town right before Thanksgiving with her brash attitude and big bulldozer, Jackson was more than a little glad to be in Belle Terre. Not even the pre-Thanksgiving excitement at the construction site, all thanks to a group of protesters that resulted in the torching of Riley's favorite bulldozer, had changed his mind.

His attention drifted momentarily as he noticed the face of a young boy peeking around the corner of the cubicle wall. He recognized the kid as the newest addition to a local family who fostered kids in transition.

"Hey, Donavan." He nodded to the kid, keeping his voice relaxed and low key.

Donavan disappeared back around the corner, but Jackson could see the tips of his sneakers at the edge of the wall. He didn't take the kid's distrust personally. Cops were the enemy to kids like Donavan. Most of the bad stuff that put them in foster care came accompanied by men and women in uniforms like his.

A huff brought his gaze back to Riley. He watched her impossibly long legs bounce like they were on springs, unable to stop his gaze from traveling up her calf to a shapely thigh. It's not like she would notice his attention. They'd come in contact only a few times since her arrival in town. Her eyes— eyes like a bottomless tropical pool he recalled from when they'd stood nose-to-forehead back at the teller's station—barely left Mr. Michel as he pecked away on his computer.

They did wander occasionally to the generous piece of pecan pie stashed near the keyboard. Her stomach grumbled, but she shifted her body and coughed behind her hand.

"It seems," the bank manager started cautiously, eyes darting over the collection of poodle pictures lining his desk to Jackson and his gun. "That the transfer was initiated on Friday afternoon but was cancelled due to lack of funds from the originating account."

Lack of funds. Jackson had heard from witnesses that she'd claimed a million dollars was missing. What was a thirty-something year old construction forewoman doing with a million dollars? His mind see-sawed between the possibilities.

Mr. Michel *harrumphed* victoriously and re-arranged the perfectly straight line of mechanical pencils with the edge of the pristine blotter. "I knew this wasn't a bank error."

Riley jabbed her finger against the desk, grazing one of

the poodle pictures and knocking it from its perfect alignment with the other pictures. "But the money was in the originating account on Friday when I initiated the transfer. Weren't you listening?" More jabbing. "It showed on my receipt, and I didn't do anything with it, so it had to be transferred as planned. It has to be lost in cyberspace somewhere." *Finger jab. Finger jab.* "Find it. *Now*."

Mr. Michel readjusted the picture, squaring his already steely posture as well.

"Patience, Ms. Kenner," Jackson advised, though he didn't feel it himself. If her accounts had been accessed illegally, it would be a major investigation. Probably federal involvement. Cybercrime was the buzz in legal circles. Not that he minded. He just didn't have the experience for that kind of thing.

It wasn't what he bargained for when he came to the sleepy town at the start of the year. And he certainly didn't expect to end up as acting sheriff before Christmas.

"I suspect Mr. Michel has more to tell you." On instinct he reached out and brushed aside the dark rope of hair from her shoulder, laying his hand on her arm. She had all that blue-black hair stuffed into a ponytail, contained but just barely. Riley Kenner wasn't a woman to be contained. At least not for long. "Give him a chance."

The grim set of her mouth tightened even further, not that it lessened the appeal of those kissable lips. She didn't pull away from his touch either so he let his fingers linger.

"Then would you please ask him to *move it along*?" She grinded out the last three words, keeping her voice low.

Riley huffed and sat back against her chair, crossing her arms. He withdrew his hand, his fingers buzzing like a hive of excited bees where they'd touched her skin. Not that much of it showed. She'd pushed the long sleeves on her t-shirt above the elbow, but they fell back down anytime she moved her arms.

The t-shirt didn't even have a daring vee neck to show the cleavage he suspected lay hidden beneath the *My eyes are higher up* logo. Well-worn jeans hugged long legs he'd noticed earlier without being painted onto her athletic frame. Each pant leg was tucked snugly into the ankle of thick-soled worker's boots.

How could so little skin turn him on this much? But it did.

Without prompting, Mr. Michel continued. "As I was saying, the transfer failed on the *other* end. The bank is not at fault here, Mrs. Kenner."

"Ms." She corrected absently before closing her eyes. Jackson could swear he heard her counting to ten under her breath. When she finally refocused her attention on the banker, a level of false calm tinged her words. "And as I said, the money showed as available on Friday. The transfer was pending on Friday. Doesn't that mean the money was there when the transfer was initiated?"

"No." Mr. Michel said, his tone edged like a cliff diver milliseconds before the fall. "It just means the transfer was initiated while the banks 'talked'." He air-quoted the word. "But the transfer didn't clear. I even show the software reini-tiated the transfer in case of error, as is protocol, but again, the transfer failed because the funds were not available in the originating account at the investment firm. Perhaps the investment firm transferred the money to another one of your accounts in error."

She scrubbed a shaking hand across her face, tucking a loose strand of midnight hair behind an ear. "I don't have any other accounts."

At least she was trying to maintain a sense of calm.

Jackson could admire the attempt. "Are you the only authorized user on the account?"

He watched the edge of desperation do a nose-dive into full-fledged panic, tracking the emotions flutter through her body. A hard swallow. The rapid blinking of her eyes. Then, finally, her body fell against the arm of the chair, away from him and Mr. Michel.

"He wouldn't do that," she said to herself, rubbing her arms unconsciously.

Curiosity pulled Jackson forward, trying to make eye contact. But her unfocused gaze didn't meet his. "Who, Riley?"

"My brother."

Damn, *she* was screwed.

Second Chance Romance is available now.

Find Second Chance Romance online.

About the Author

Maggie Preston is an award-winning author of contemporary romantic fiction. She fell in love with romance before she knew what it was, stealing paperback novels from her grandmother's closet when her mother wasn't looking.

She loves to travel and tells people that anything and everything they do could end up in her next novel, so if you recognize yourself in the pages of her books, remember you were warned.

Maggie currently balances her life between the right brain and left brain, quality consultant and technical writer by day, romance writer by night.

www.AuthorMaggiePreston.com

Follow Maggie on Social Media

Also by Maggie Preston

Hearts of Louisiana

Second Chance Romance

Love and Miss Fortune

Hearts of Carolina Anthology

Two If by Sea

Back Home Again Anthology

Dance of the Butterflies